# The master of St. Benedict's
## Vol. 1

*by*

Alan St. Aubyn

# The master of St. Benedict's
## Vol. 1

**by Alan St. Aubyn**




ISBN: 978-93-63056-72-5

**Published by**

# DOUBLE 9 BOOKS

2/13-B, Ansari Road
Daryaganj, New Delhi – 110002
info@double9books.com
www.double9books.com
Tel. 011-40042856

# ABOUT THE AUTHOR

Alan St. Aubyn, a literary virtuoso of his time, penned the timeless masterpiece "The Master of St. Benedict's." In this captivating novel, St. Aubyn intricately weaves together a tale of intrigue, ambition, and redemption set against the backdrop of a prestigious English boarding school. Through rich character development and evocative prose, St. Aubyn brings to life the world of St. Benedict's, where tradition and modernity collide, and secrets lurk behind every ivy-covered wall. At the heart of the story is the enigmatic figure of the Master, whose unwavering dedication to the school's legacy is tested by personal turmoil and external pressures. As the narrative unfolds, readers are drawn into a web of complex relationships, moral dilemmas, and hidden agendas, culminating in a gripping climax that leaves a lasting impression. With its timeless themes and masterful storytelling, "The Master of St. Benedict's" stands as a testament to St. Aubyn's literary prowess and his ability to captivate readers with tales of human resilience and the search for meaning in a rapidly changing world.

# CONTENTS

# CHAPTER I
# FULL OF DAYS, RICHES, AND HONOUR

The Master of St. Benedict's had got as much out of life as most men. His had been a longer life than is allotted to many men—it had exceeded four score.

There had been room in these eight decades for all the things that men desire: for ambition, for wealth, for the world's favour, for success—well-earned success—and for love. There had also been distinction, and the soft, delightful voice of praise had not been silent.

The success and the distinction had come early in life, and the love had come late. In the nature of things it could not have come earlier. It came in time to crown the rest of the good gifts that Providence had poured into the lap of the Master of St. Benedict's. It had been his already for twenty years, and it was his still. Surely we are right in saying that he had got as much out of life as most men?

He had begun life on a bleak Yorkshire moor, following the plough over his father's fields. A kindly North Riding vicar, noting the boy's taste for reading, and his inaptitude for the drudgery of the farm, had placed him at his own cost at the grammar school of the adjoining town. With a small scholarship the Yorkshire ploughboy came up to Cambridge. He came up with a very few loose coins in the pocket of his homely-cut clothes, and with a broad North-country dialect as barbarous as the cut of his coat.

He was the butt of all the witty men of St. Benedict's during his freshman's year. He was the subject of all the rough practical jokes which undergraduates in old days were wont to play upon impecunious youths who had the audacity to elbow them out of the highest places in the examinations.

He had survived the practical jokes, and he had stayed 'up' when the witty men had gone 'down.' He had won the highest honours of his year, and in due course he had been promoted to a college Fellowship. Everything had come in delightful sequence: honour, riches, distinction, love. It had all fallen out exactly as he would have had it to fall out. He might have liked the love to have come earlier—he had waited for it forty years: it came at sixty, and he had enjoyed it for over twenty years!

When Anthony Rae had come up to Cambridge, a poor scholar from a country grammar school, he had set before himself two things that seemed at the time equally impossible. He had set before himself the winning of a high place, perhaps the highest, among the great scholars of his great University, and he had also set before himself—in his secret heart—the hope of winning, to share this distinction with him, the daughter of the kind friend who had paved the way to distinction and honour.

He had achieved both these things—the dearest wishes of his heart—but he had to serve a longer apprenticeship than most men. He had to wait forty years.

Rachel Thorne was worth waiting for. She was a child when he went away to college; she had run down to the Vicarage gate after him on that memorable morning to wish him 'good luck,' and she had stood watching him until a turn of the road hid him from her eyes.

She had watched for him turning that corner many times since. She had met him at the gate of the dear old Yorkshire Vicarage when he came back, term after term, a modest undergraduate blushing beneath his well-earned honours, with the eager question on her lips: 'What great things, have you done this term, Anthony?'

She always expected him to do great things, and he justified her faith in him. Perhaps her girlish faith had more to do with his success than he dreamed of. It was his beacon through all his lonely hours, and it had led him onward to distinction and honour.

She was brown-haired and fresh-cheeked when he went away; she was a middle-aged woman, with silver streaks in her brown hair, when he came back and asked her to share with him the honours he had won.

She waited for him through all the long years of his Fellowship—sad years when fortune had left her and sorrow had baptized her—sad friendless years, growing older, and grayer, and sick with waiting. But the reward had come at last, and her tranquil face had regained its cheerfulness, and was 'no longer wan and dree.'

It was a fitting crown to a scholarly life, this mellow, mature love—this gracious presence pervading the closing decades of his brilliant career.

Rachel Rae had been mistress of St. Benedict's over twenty years when our story opens. She had presided over the graceful hospitalities of the Master's lodge in her kindly, gracious way for twenty years. She had no daughter to share this delightful duty with her—she had married too late in life—but a niece of the Master's had been an inmate of the lodge for fifteen years or more, and filled a daughter's place.

Mary Rae was a daughter of a younger brother of Dr. Rae's, and had been educated above the station in which she had been born by her uncle's liberality. Anthony Rae in his prosperity had not neglected his humble kinsfolk. He had done as much for them as lay in his power. He had educated the younger branches, and provided for the declining years of the elders. He had kept his two maiden sisters, one an invalid, in comfort and affluence. He had paid the mortgage off the farm and passed it over unembarrassed by debt to his elder brother. He had taken that brother's grandson and given him an education at his own University, and in due time had arranged for him to be presented with a college living. It was not a rich living: it was the only one that fell vacant when Richard Rae most wanted it, and he had accepted it gladly. He had married upon it, and brought up a family, six children, of whom one only was now living, a girl child, with whom this story has to do.

The old Master of St. Benedict's had aged perceptibly within the last few years. He was already in his second childhood. His strength had become enfeebled and his memory impaired. He could not walk down the long gallery of the lodge now or across the grass in the Fellows' garden without assistance; he could not remember the things of yesterday or of last week, but the crabbed characters of his old Semitic manuscripts were still as familiar to him as ever. He had lost a great deal since that stroke of paralysis five years ago, but he had not lost all. He remembered his old friends, and he could pore over his old books, but he was dependent upon his womankind for many things—for most things.

Mary Rae opened his letters and conducted his correspondence. She had conducted it so long that she knew more about the college than the Master. She transacted all the college business that had to be transacted in the lodge, and when any public function required the Master's presence in the Senate House Mary Rae took him up to the door on her arm and brought him back. It was also rumoured that she instructed him how to vote.

She was assisted in her responsible duties by the Senior Tutor of St. Benedict's, who would in the natural course of things succeed to the office of Master when it should fall vacant.

Mary Rae was a handsome woman well on in the thirties. She was a woman who could not help looking handsome at any age, and the few gray hairs that had put in an appearance in the smooth brown bands drawn back from her broad forehead only added a new dignity to her mature beauty.

Perhaps the Senior Tutor thought that they supplied the only touch lacking to make Mary Rae a perfect and ideal mistress of a college lodge.

It was whispered in the combination room, where the old Fellows met after their Hall dinner, and discussed the affairs of the college over their walnuts and their wine, that when the Master received his last preferment she would not have to pack up her small belongings and leave the lodge.

It was one morning early in the Lent term that Mary Rae sat at breakfast in the cheerful bow-windowed room of the lodge. The Doctor's wife still presided over the breakfast table. She was younger than the Doctor, and had worn better. She was still active and cheerful—a bright, gentle, patient old soul, ever watchful and considerate for his comfort, and anticipating his every want.

While Mrs. Rae poured out the Master's tea, Mary Rae buttered the Master's toast and read his letters. There were not many letters this morning, but there was one with a black seal that lay uppermost. The writing was unfamiliar, and before opening it Mary glanced at the postmark.

'A letter from Dick, uncle,' she said across the table. She had to speak in rather a high key, as the Doctor was a little deaf, and some days he was deafer than usual.

'What does Dick say, my dear?' he said, smiling at her across the toast she had buttered for him. His voice was not very strong, but there was no North-country burr in it now—a kind, mellow old voice, courteous and gentle in tone, with a quaver in it now and then. 'I have not heard from your uncle Dick for a long time. I am very glad he has written now. I cannot remember when I last heard from him.'

'It is not from Uncle Dick,' said Mary, opening the letter; 'it is from his son—at least, his grandson—Cousin Dick, of Thorpe Regis. Don't you remember, uncle?'

'Ye—es, my dear; and what does Dick say?'

Mary read the letter in silence, and looked across the table with a shade of anxiety on her face.

'It is not Cousin Dick who writes; the letter is from his daughter; he had only one daughter—Lucy, little Lucy. You remember her, uncle?'

Mary Rae was evidently speaking to gain time, and the shade of anxiety deepened on her face as she spoke.

'Ye—es, I remember, my dear. Lucy was her mother's name; she was called after her mother. What has Lucy got to say about Dick?'

'She has not much to say, uncle; she is writing in great distress. Her father has died, almost suddenly. He was preaching a week ago, and now he is dead. The poor child is writing in great trouble.'

'Dick dead!' the old man repeated with a bewildered air, and putting down his cup with a shaking hand. 'Dick dead, did you say? He was not so many years older than I, and always hale and strong. I ought to have gone first. There were only three of us, and Dick was the eldest.'

'It isn't your brother, Anthony, that is dead; he died long ago, dear. It is his grandson, little Dick—Dickie you used to call him. You had him up here, and he took his degree, and you gave him a college living. You remember little Dickie, Anthony?'

His wife's voice recalled his wandering thoughts.

'Yes, yes, my dear; certainly, I remember little Dick very well. He took a second class; he ought to have done better. He disappointed me. I had no son of my own to come after me, and I should have liked my brother Dick's son—grandson, to be sure—to have done well. He did his best, no doubt; but he disappointed me. If he had done better, he might have got a Fellowship. So Dickie is dead, you say, my dear?'

'Yes, uncle; and he has left poor little Lucy unprovided for. She has written to ask you what she ought to do. She wants to go out as a governess—a nursery governess.'

'A nursery governess? Dick's little girl a nursery governess! No, my dear, that will never do. Tell her to come here; there's plenty of room in the lodge for Dick's little girl. Write to her at once, Mary, and tell her as soon— as soon as the funeral is over—her father's funeral—poor little girl!—to come to the lodge. What do you say, Rachel?'

'I wish we could spare Mary to go to her,' the Master's wife said, wiping her eyes. 'Someone ought to fetch her away at once, as soon—as soon as it is all over. I think Mary ought to go to her.'

The Senior Tutor met the Master's niece in the court as he was coming away from a lecture during the morning, and she told him all about the letter her uncle had received and the death of his nephew, or, rather, his grand-nephew.

'You remember my cousin Dick?' she said; 'he was my second cousin. I am a generation older than he,' and she smiled at the admission. She was not the least ashamed of her age.

The Senior Tutor smiled too; he was thinking how well she wore her years, how her age, or the signs of it, her gray hairs and the lines on her face, became her. She would grow handsomer with the years, he told himself as he stood talking to her in the spring sunshine, and her face would grow finer as time went by: it was a fine face already; it could never by any chance grow plain. He had watched a great many faces grow old in his time—old, and lined, and soured—but he had never seen any face grow finer with the years like this woman's face had grown.

'Yes,' he said, 'I remember your cousin, Richard Rae, very well; he was one of my pupils. He disappointed me, and he disappointed your uncle; he ought to have taken a first class. He went into the Church, and we gave him a college living, I remember—a very small living—and he married, I believe, directly after.'

'He married, and he had a large family and a sickly wife, and very small means. It must have been a hard struggle for him, poor Dick! He lost his wife, and his children died one after the other; there is only one left. And now he is dead, and the girl is left quite alone.'

'Oh, it is a girl,' said the Tutor in a tone of disappointment; 'if it had been a boy we could have done something with him here.'

'Yes,' said Mary, with a sigh; 'pity it's a girl; it would have been so much easier if it had been a boy. She must come here, of course; there is nowhere else for her to go.'

'What will you do with her when she comes?'

The Senior Tutor looked grave; the question had come into his head as he stood speaking to Mary, what should he do with this girl of Cousin Dick's when he occupied the Master's place? Of course Mary would stay, and Mrs. Rae—he could not separate the old woman from her niece during her few declining years; she would certainly remain an inmate of the lodge; but this girl? he could not make the college lodge an asylum for all the female members of the Rae family.

It was an idiotic question to arise; he was ashamed of it the next moment.

'I think you ought to go to Thorpe Regis,' he said, 'and be with your poor young cousin at this trying time. I will look after the Master while you are away, if that will make the going easier.'

'Ye—es,' said Mary slowly, 'it will make it easier. You really think I ought to go?'

There was a hesitation in her tone he could not but note; he put it down at once to her reluctance to leave the old Master.

'Most certainly you ought to go,' he said promptly. 'I will come over to the lodge every day. I will fill your place as far as I can. You are not afraid to leave the Master with me?'

'Oh, no, no! I am sure you will do all, more than all, that I do for him. I was not thinking about him. You are quite sure it is right to bring this girl back here? She is very young, not twenty, and—and she may be— —'

'She may be attractive,' said the Senior Tutor with a laugh, 'and turn all our heads. I think, in spite of her attractions, her place is here with you and under her uncle's roof. We must protect ourselves against the wiles of this siren. We must not wear our hearts on our sleeves for Cousin Dick's little daughter to peck at.'

# CHAPTER II
# DICK'S LITTLE DAUGHTER

The Senior Tutor need have been under no apprehension for the men of St. Benedict's. They had no occasion to cover up their sleeves with their academical gowns. Cousin Dick's little daughter showed no inclination to peck at their too susceptible hearts, whether they wore them skewered on to their sleeves or out of sight in their accustomed places.

Lucy Rae was too full of her recent loss, the great sorrow that had fallen upon her and swept away all her household gods, to have a thought to spare for the undergraduates of St. Benedict's.

It had almost swept away all her moorings, too, but not quite; she still clung tenaciously to one idea—it was all she had left of the old life to cling to: she still desired to be a governess.

It was not a very ambitious idea. She wanted to be independent, and earn her own living in the only way that was open to her. She accepted the shelter of the Master's lodge thankfully, but she had no idea of settling down in the dependent position of a poor relation. When she had recovered from this shock, and the horizon cleared, she would find something to do, she told herself, and go away.

She was a soft, shy little thing to be so independent. She only looked like a girl to be kissed and petted and comforted; she didn't look at all fit to stand in the front of the battle.

She talked over her prospects—her little, humble prospects—with her cousin Mary a few days after her arrival at the lodge. Mary was sitting at the Master's writing-table in the library of the lodge—she was writing some letters on college business—and Lucy was sewing in the window.

It was a big gloomy room, and it was not at all a cheerful place for girls to sit in on a chilly spring afternoon. There was a fire burning in the old-fashioned grate behind the brass fire-guard—there were wire guards to all the fires at the lodge since that last seizure of the Master's—but it had burnt low; Mary, who was sitting near it, had been too occupied to notice it, and Lucy's mind was full of her prospects.

There had been no sound in the room for some time but the scratching of Mary's pen as it travelled over the paper, and Lucy sewed on in silence. She didn't like sewing, and she put down her work two or three times and yawned or looked out of the window. The window looked out into the Fellows' garden. The sun was shining on the lawn beneath, which was already green with the new green of the year, and the crocuses were aflame in the borders, and the primroses were in bloom.

An old Fellow was hobbling slowly and painfully round the garden—a bent, drooping figure in a particularly shabby coat and a tall silk hat of a bygone date. He was lame, Lucy remarked, and dragged one leg behind him. He had a long, lean, sallow face with deep eye-sockets, and his hair was long and gray—it didn't look as if it had been cut for years. Lucy wondered vaguely at seeing this shabby old cripple in the grounds of the lodge; if she had seen him anywhere else she would have taken him for a tramp. He had been a Senior Wrangler in his day, and had taken a double-first; perhaps he was paying the penalty.

'I am very dull company, child,' Mary said, as she blotted her last letter and pushed the writing materials aside. 'I have left you to your thoughts for a whole hour, and we have sat the fire out. What have you been thinking about, Lucy, all this time?'

'Oh, the old thing,' said Lucy, looking up from her work. 'I have been thinking what I can do.'

'Well, and what conclusion have you come to?'

'There is but one conclusion—that—that I can do nothing!'

The work dropped from the girl's fingers, and her eyes overflowed. She had wanted an excuse for weeping for the last hour, and now she had got it.

'Oh yes, you can,' Mary said cheerfully; 'the case is not quite so bad as that. You can sew, for one thing. See how nicely you are sewing that frill!'

'I hate sewing! And I shall never wear that frill when I have hemmed it! I can only do useless trumpery things!'

Lucy let the poor little bit of white frilling she had been hemming fall to the ground, and she got up and began to walk up and down the room.

Mary watched her in silence. It was not the first time her young cousin had shown impatience, but it was the first time she had shown temper—just a little bit of temper.

Mary had praised her in the wrong place: she was hurt and angry at this learned, superior cousin implying, with her misplaced praise, that she was only fit to do work—mere woman's work!

It was an unusual sound, that rapid pacing to and fro of impatient feet, in that scholarly room. The Master tottered feebly across the floor; the Master's wife moved with slow dignity; Mary walked quietly, with soft, firm footsteps that awoke no echoes. The floor creaked audibly beneath Lucy's rapid, impatient steps; the old boards that had echoed to the slow tread of scholars for so many, many years, shook and trembled—actually trembled—beneath the light impatient footsteps of Cousin Dick's little daughter.

The colour that that useless sewing had taken out of Lucy's cheek had come back, and her gray eyes were eager and shining beneath her tears.

Mary watched her pacing the room with a smile half of pity, half amused, as she sat at the Master's table. Perhaps she understood the mood. She may have been impatient herself years ago; she had nothing to be impatient for now. Everything was happening as it should do; and when a change came— well, her position would not be materially altered.

'I am sure you can do a great many useful things, dear,' she said presently, when Lucy's little bit of temper had had time to cool. 'You could not have kept your father's house so long, and done the work of the parish, without being able to do more useful things than most girls.'

'I don't mean that kind of usefulness; anyone can do housekeeping and potter about a parish. I hated parish work! I never took the least interest in it; no one could have done it worse than I did. I hated—oh, no one knows how I hated—those Bands of Hope, and Sunday-schools, and mothers' meetings, and visiting dreadful old men and women who would insist upon telling me all about their unpleasant complaints!'

Mary looked grave. She was accustomed to hear a great deal about old people's complaints, though she did not do any district visiting.

'Really,' she said gravely, 'most girls like these things! They are over now, and done with, and you will begin afresh. Tell me what you would like to do.'

'Like!' Lucy held her breath as she spoke, and her cheeks grew crimson. 'Oh, I should like to be a scholar, Cousin Mary!'

Mary looked at the girl with a kind of pity in her eyes. She had seen a good many scholars in her time, men and women; some of them were as eager once as this girl—eager and impatient with feverish haste to climb the hill of learning; they were hollow-eyed now, and narrow-chested, and their cheeks were sunken and sallow, and some limped like the old scholar in the

Fellows' garden—that is, those who had lasted to the end; but some had turned back in time and regained their youth: most likely this girl would turn back.

'You would like to go to a woman's college?'

'I should love to go! I shouldn't mind whether it were Newnham or Girton, whichever uncle thought best. If I could only have three years at a woman's college, I should be provided for for life. I should want nothing further. I should be able to make my own way. Oh, Mary, do you think he will let me go?'

She was very much in earnest. She had stopped running up and down the room in that ridiculous manner. She was standing beside the table with both her hands pressed down upon it and her little lithe figure bending eagerly forward. Her eyes were shining, and her cheeks glowing, and her lips parted. She looked exactly as if she were making a speech.

The door opened as she was standing there, and the Senior Tutor came in. He shook hands with Mary, and he nodded across the table to Lucy. He thought he had interrupted a scene.

'I saw the Master as I came up,' he said, speaking to Mary; 'he had just finished his nap. He asked me to tell you that he was quite ready to take a turn in the garden, if you would put on your hat. I think you should go at once to catch the sunshine. You'll get it on the broad walk if you go now.'

Mary rose at once.

'It is lucky I have finished my work,' she said, glancing down at the little pile of letters, sealed and stamped ready for the post, that lay on the table. 'Poor little Lucy here was telling me about her plans. If you can spare time, Mr. Colville, sit down and talk them over with her, and advise her what she ought to do, while I am in the garden.'

The Senior Tutor could spare time; and after he had opened the door for Mary, he came back to the window that overlooked the garden and sat down.

He did not belong to the old school of Cambridge Dons. He belonged to that newer school that came in a quarter of a century ago with athletics. He was not lean and hollow-eyed, and wrinkled and yellow, like a musty old parchment, and he hadn't a stoop in his shoulders, and he didn't drag one of his legs behind him. He had rowed 'five' in his college boat, and his shoulders were as square now as ever. His shoulders were square, and his forehead was square, and his iron-gray hair was closely cut—it was only iron-gray still—and he had tremendous bushy eyebrows that, Lucy thought, made him look like an ogre, and that frightened the undergraduates dreadfully, and close-cut iron-gray whiskers, and a big red throat like a bull. His throat had not always been red; he had been mild-looking enough in his youth; but he was now a portly, pompous Don of middle age, with a florid countenance and fierce aspect.

'Well,' he said in his easy, patronizing way, as if he were speaking to a freshman who had just come up, 'and what do you propose to do, Miss Lucy?'

The colour went out of the girl's cheeks, and the long eyelashes drooped over her eager eyes, and her pretty little slender figure grew limp, and she didn't look the least like making a speech now.

'I am sure I don't know,' she said meekly, and she went back and sat on her old seat in the window on the opposite side to the Senior Tutor. It was a big bay-window, and there was a table between them littered with pamphlets and manuscripts in Semitic languages. The girl tossed them over as she sat there with a gesture of impatience. They were sealed books to her.

'What were you discussing with your cousin Ma—ry when I came in?'

He lingered over the name, and prolonged the last syllable. He seemed loath to let it go.

'I was telling her that I should like to go to a woman's college—to Newnham or Girton.'

'Exactly.'

The Tutor nodded his head. He was listening to the girl, but he was looking out of the window.

'No one is educated now—no woman—who does not go to Newnham, or Girton, or Oxford. No one has any chance of success in teaching who has not taken a place in a Tripos or done something in a University examination.'

The Senior Tutor was smiling, but he was only giving her half his attention.

'And what Tripos do you propose to take?' he asked in his bland, superior, lecture-room manner.

'I? Oh, I don't think I shall ever be clever enough to take a Tripos; but I might learn something—a little. I might learn enough to pass the—the— Little——'

'The Little-go?' suggested the Tutor; 'or, more properly speaking, the "Previous."'

'Yes; papa used to talk about the Little-go. He had dreadful difficulty in passing it. I should be quite satisfied if I could pass the Little-go.'

'I don't think you will find any difficulty in passing it,' he said. 'I do not remember that your father had any special difficulty; I was his tutor. He disappointed me in the Tripos. With his great gifts he ought to have done better.'

It was Lucy's turn to smile now, and to sigh.

'Poor papa!' she said; 'there was a reason for his failure. Perhaps you did not know.'

'No; I knew of no reason.'

'He had just met my mother, and—and he was in love. She got between him and his mathematics; he could think of nothing but my mother. Oh, if you had known her, you would not have wondered.'

The Senior Tutor looked across the table with a new interest in his eyes at the sweet downcast face. If her mother had been like her, he didn't wonder at poor Richard Rae getting only a second class in his Tripos.

'Are you quite sure that you will not fail from the same cause? are you sure that at the momentous time you will not do like your father—that you will not fall in love?'

'No—o,' said Lucy gravely; 'I don't think I shall fall in love. I don't think Girton girls do very often.'

'They do sometimes. They generally end by marrying their coaches.'

Lucy looked shocked.

'They can't *all* marry their coaches.'

'No, not all—only the weak ones. The superior minds never sink to the low level of matrimony.'

Lucy was quite sure he was laughing at her.

'I am not likely to need a coach,' she said stiffly; 'I shall never be clever enough to take a Tripos. I shall be content to pass the—the—the "Previous."'

She was going to say 'Little-go,' but she remembered he had called it the 'Previous,' and she checked herself in time.

'We shall see. You will have to begin with the "Previous" in any case. You need not take it all at once: there are three parts; you can take them at different times.'

'I should prefer to take them all at once.'

'But if you are going no farther, if you are going to stop at the "Previous," why should you be in such a hurry to get it over?'

'I don't know. It might be as well to get it over; but I have to get into Girton or Newnham first; I don't know that they will have me; and I have to get my uncle's consent.'

She hadn't fallen naturally into the custom of the lodge of calling Dr. Rae 'the Master' yet. It came easier to say 'uncle.'

'There will be an entrance examination,' the Tutor said, looking out of window and watching the Master walking in the garden below leaning on Mary's arm. 'I believe it is nearly as stiff as the "Previous" and takes in the same subjects. You will have to pass an examination before you can become a student at either college.'

'Do you know what the subjects are?' she asked eagerly; 'could you— could you get me the papers?'

He hardly heard her; his heart was out in that wet garden with Mary. How very indiscreet of the Master at his age to walk over the damp grass! He was actually sitting down on the bench under the walnut-tree. Lucy followed the direction of the Tutor's eyes, but she only saw the Master sitting in the sunshine. A tall, lean figure bent with age, with white, silvery hair falling over the velvet collar of his coat, and his rugged, worn old face turned up to the sun. The figure of the old scholar sitting on the old bench in the sunshine beneath the branches of the old, old tree, where he had sat in sunshine and in shade, oh, so many, many years, had no poetry for her. She only wondered, as she saw him sitting there, lifting his dim eyes to the sinking sun, whether he would let her go to Newnham.

The Senior Tutor didn't see any poetry in the situation, either. He was sure the old Master was catching a dreadful cold; and he was wondering whether Mary had changed her slippers.

'Could you get me a copy of the papers set at the last examination?' Lucy asked meekly.

'Yes, oh yes,' he said absently; 'I'll try to remember; but I think I must go down now and bring the Master in: I am sure he is taking cold.'

# CHAPTER III
# ONLY A FRESHER

It was rather hard work to persuade the old Master of St. Benedict's that Lucy ought to go to Newnham. He belonged to the old school—he was almost the last left of that school—that did not believe very much in women. He believed in a girl learning to sew, and to spell, and play a little air on the piano—he was very fond of 'Annie Laurie,' he could listen to it by the hour; he went so far, indeed, as the three R's in a woman's education—and he stopped there.

He had no sympathy whatever in the movement for the higher education of Women—spelt with a big W. He had voted consistently all his life against women being admitted to any of the privileges of the University, against their being allowed to take degrees; he had even voted against their being 'placed.' He regarded every concession made to the weaker sex as a step towards that dreadful time when a female Vice-Chancellor will confer degrees in the Senate House, and a lady D.D. will occupy the University pulpit.

With these views, and with his prejudices growing stronger rather than weaker with the years, it was no wonder that Mary Rae had great difficulty in reconciling the Master to the idea of Lucy becoming a student of Newnham.

He had to look at the question all round, from every point of view, and he had to talk it over a great many times. Sometimes he talked it over with himself after dinner, when he woke up from his nap, or didn't quite wake up; and sometimes he talked it over with his nieces.

'I don't think your father would approve of it, my dear,' he said one day when he was talking 'it' over with Lucy. 'He was a plain man, he hadn't the advantages of education that I had; but he had what served him just as well, he had common-sense. He knew what was wanted in a woman. A woman, he used to say, ought to be able to milk, and make butter, and bring up a family. Dick's wife could do all these, and her poultry was noted in all the country round.'

Lucy sighed. She had no ambition to make butter and bring up a family, and she had a distinct aversion to poultry. She hated cocks and hens and broods of yellow downy chickens. She remembered how they used always to be getting into the Vicarage garden and digging up her flower-seeds.

'I am afraid I couldn't get my living by making butter, uncle,' she said meekly, 'or milking cows.'

She never could remember to say 'Master,' like everybody else.

'No, my dear, no; I suppose not. Some girls have the knack of it, and some women, I've heard my mother say, may churn for hours and the butter will refuse to come. Dick's wife, your mother, my dear——'

'Great-grandmother,' murmured Lucy almost inaudibly. The Master hated to be contradicted, and he was always telling her that these far-off ancestors were her father and mother, this humble ploughman and his homely wife. There had been two generations of culture between, and Lucy had quite forgotten, until her uncle reminded her, that her great-grandmother used to carry her eggs and her butter to market. The worst of it was he used to tell everybody it was her mother.

'Yes, yes,' the Master repeated testily; 'my memory is not what it was. But it does not much matter which. She was a good woman; she did her duty here; she brought up a long family—nine children—and she has gone to her reward. She did not know a word of Greek or Latin, and she only knew enough mathematics to reckon up the price of eggs; but if she had gone to Girton or Newnham she could not have done more. She did her duty here; after all, that is the great thing, my dear. There is nothing else that will bring comfort at the last.'

It was a delightful reflection. It comforted the old scholar who had done his duty in this place for over sixty years, who had done it so well that by common consent men called him Master; but it didn't comfort Lucy at all. She was quite prepared to do her duty, only she wanted to do it in her own way.

There were other difficulties in the way of Lucy going to Newnham beside the Master's prejudices. There was a dreadful ordeal to be gone through before those sacred portals would be opened to admit her.

There was the entrance examination. The Senior Tutor was as good as his word; he brought Lucy over the very next day, not only the papers set at the last 'Previous' examination, but a copy of the last Newnham entrance papers. The next examination was to take place in March, and it was now the middle of February, and there were only a few weeks to prepare for it.

Lucy looked hurriedly through the papers while the Tutor stood by, and he saw her face fall and the pretty April colour, which was Lucy's especial charm, go out of her cheeks.

'They are stiffer than you thought,' he said.

He couldn't help putting a little feeling into his voice; he couldn't help being sorry for the girl. He could see she was dreadfully disappointed.

'I did not think they would be so hard,' she said, with something like a sob, and striving to keep back the tears; 'I had no idea that so much was required.'

Her voice was scarcely steady, and she finished up with a little wail— she couldn't keep it out of her voice—and she laid the papers down.

'You don't think you can do them?'

'No, I am sure I can't.'

'Not if you work hard—very hard?—you have three weeks before you—not if I help you?'

'You! Oh, Mr. Colville!'

The colour leaped back into her face, and her eyes brightened. She was quite trembling with eagerness.

'If you think with three weeks' hard work you can get through, I will help you,' he said.

It was something new to the Senior Tutor to have a pupil so eager and willing. The eyes of the undergraduates of St. Benedict's were not accustomed to brighten or their cheeks to flush when he proposed to give them a few hours' extra coaching.

'I am sure I can!' she said eagerly; 'and—and you are sure, Mr. Colville, you will not mind the trouble? I am a very slow learner, but I will do my best, my very best.'

'I am sure you will,' he said; and then he noticed that little helpless quivering about her lips that touched him with quite a new sensation. He had never seen Mary's lips quiver. 'It will be no trouble,' the Tutor said softly in quite a different voice; he even noticed the difference himself, with a strange sense of wonder. 'I shall be very glad to be of use to you.'

He had often been of use to Mary. She always consulted him about the college business; she made use of him every day; but his voice had never faltered nor his cheek grown warm when he had offered to help her with the Master's correspondence.

Lucy began her work the next day. She turned out from the little shabby box she had brought with her to the lodge some well-thumbed old schoolbooks. Small as the box was, it contained all her personal belongings, and the books were at the bottom of the box.

Like Jacob, she had come into a strange land with very little personal impedimenta. It could all, everything, be stuffed into one small box, and the books were at the bottom. The books were shabby, like the box. They had belonged to her father, and she had read them with him.

There were his old Virgil and Xenophon, and a dilapidated Euclid with all the riders missing, and an old-fashioned Algebra. There had been newer editions since Richard Rae had used these in his college days more than twenty years ago. There had been delightful editions full of notes, and directing-posts along the royal road to a classical education; but Lucy had been plodding along the old, rough, dusty way.

The Senior Tutor smiled as he turned over these old books. They brought back to him the old days twenty years ago, the hopes and dreams of those early days, and the familiar faces. The dreams had been realized — at least, some of them — but the familiar faces had faded with the years, and the hopes — what could a man hope for beyond being Master of his college? Nevertheless, the Senior Tutor sighed. The sight of these old books had carried him a long way back.

'I think we can find some newer editions than these,' he said, smiling.

He not only found some newer, but he found the very newest. He found delightful books that smoothed away all the difficulties and made stony places plain. There will be a royal road to learning by-and-by. The road is getting smoother every day, and the way is getting shorter — a short, straight, macadamized road that one can travel over without any jolting or sudden pulls-up.

Old scholars who remember the dear old rough road, and the stony ways, and the hills of difficulty they had to climb, sigh when they look back. There is no time now, in these hurrying days, to toil over stones and climb unnecessary heights. The new ways are so much better than the old; but the old men, if they were to begin again, would go the old way, the dear old way, with all its difficulties. They will still tell you the old ways are best.

Lucy Rae was not a scholar yet, though the desire of her heart was to be one — a perfect Hypatia — and the new royal road was exactly what she wanted.

She made such rapid progress by means of these short-cuts and easy paths the Senior Tutor led her through that she was quite ready for that dreaded entrance examination when it came. She did as well in it as the girls who had been working for it for years.

There was nothing now to prevent her becoming a student of Newnham. Cousin Mary had talked the old Master over and smoothed away all the difficulties. She had wrung from him an unwilling consent. The Senior Tutor had done his part, too, in overcoming the Master's prejudices. He had backed Mary up in the most loyal manner; no girl could have had better advocates. When the Doctor had urged that there had been no precedent in his family of girls construing Latin and Greek when they ought to be making butter and carrying their eggs to market, the Tutor had reminded him that neither had there been a precedent in all the generations of the Raes of one of their number being the Master of a college.

He, on his part, had set up a precedent, and Dick's little daughter was going to set up another—perhaps a more astonishing precedent.

Lucy Rae went up to Newnham the next term. She ought to have waited until October, when the academical year commences, but she was much too anxious to begin at once. She couldn't wait till October.

She had taken a little draught of the divine nectar, and she was thirsting to drink deeply, ever so deeply—deeper than any woman had ever drunk yet. She was going to do very big things, and she couldn't afford to lose a minute. She would gain a whole term's work if she went up now, she would get in ten terms' work instead of nine, like the men, for her Tripos. She would get a whole term's start of them.

With this thirst upon her, and this emulation stirring in her heart, Lucy packed her little box and carried it up to Newnham. She did not exactly carry it in her arms like a housemaid going to a new place. It was not far to carry it, and for the weight of it she might have carried it easily, but girls do not generally go to Newnham carrying a bandbox, or a bundle tied up in a coloured pocket-handkerchief, and with two out-at-elbow little brothers lagging behind carrying a shabby box between them. Lucy, alas! had not two out-at-elbow little brothers, and she had respect for the feelings of Newnham, so she drove up to the door of Newe Hall in a hansom, with her modest little box on the roof.

She thought it was the happiest, the proudest day of her life, this first day at Newnham. She had been looking forward to it for weeks. She had lain awake all the night before picturing what it would be like, and it was not the least like anything she had pictured.

She had pictured sunshine and a blue sky, and the lilacs in the hedge budding, and the daffodils blowing beneath the windows. It was the middle of April, and she had a right to expect these things; it was very little to expect.

It had been raining cheerfully all the morning, and it was raining still when the hansom drew up at the gate of St. Benedict's; it couldn't draw up at the door of the lodge, because college lodges are cut off from the outside world by cloistered courts, and even royalty, when it visits the master of a college, has to leave its carriage at the gate and perform the rest of the journey on foot.

Lucy met Mr. Colville in the cloisters as she was hurrying through, and he put her into the hansom, and he told the man where to drive, and quite a crowd of undergraduates, who had come up early in the term, stood round the gate watching her drive away.

It was quite a new thing, a girl going from St. Benedict's to Newnham. It was the newest thing under the sun. No daughter, niece or granddaughter of any Master of St. Benedict's had ever driven from those gates before to Newnham.

Perhaps when there is a mixed University, and a female president at the lodge, they will not have to go so far; they may find rooms beneath the same roof.

Who shall say?

Lucy couldn't have driven away with more depressing surroundings. The sky couldn't have been grayer, and the trees were shivering overhead, and the hedges were dripping, and there was a nasty mist settling down over everything. She forgot all about the lilacs and the daffodils she had been picturing as she stood, a forlorn little black figure, in the big, cheerless vestibule of Newe Hall, paying the driver of the hansom. There was no one at Newnham to receive her, no one to show her to her room, only a housemaid, who went away directly she reached the door. She didn't even open the door of the room; she only pointed to it and went away in another direction.

It was a little bare room, it couldn't have been barer. There was a couch that served for a bed, a bureau with some drawers beneath, a table, a couple of chairs, and a thinly disguised washstand with imperfect crockery; and that was all. Unless, indeed, a chintz curtain drawn across a corner of the room for hanging gowns behind could be called a wardrobe.

There was no fire, and the barred windows were steaming and blurred with the mist outside, and the raw spring afternoon was closing in.

Lucy shivered and looked round the desolate room. She didn't know what she was expected to do next, or how she was to begin this new life. She was a member of the University now, she told herself with bated breath; she was really a female undergraduate, and she had got to begin as undergraduates began.

Should she begin with lighting the fire? While she was debating this point, and drawing off her gloves, a girl came in. She had left the door open so that anyone passing could look in and see her standing there, and the girl passing by looked in and saw her, and something in her attitude touched her, and she came in. Perhaps it was her black frock and her white face.

'Can I do anything for you?' she said. She didn't throw any sympathy into her voice; they never do at Newnham. 'I've got a kettle boiling if you'd like some water, or'—looking round the bare room and seeing that Lucy's things were not unpacked—'perhaps you'd rather have some tea.'

'Ye—es,' Lucy said quite thankfully; 'I would rather have some tea, please.'

'Then come into my room.'

Lucy followed the girl, a solid-looking girl with no profile to speak of, and a turned-up nose and violent red hair. She had not to follow her far, only across the passage.

There was a card slipped into a frame in the door of the room, and the name of the occupant was written on it—'Stubbs.'

'That's my name,' said the girl, pointing to it; 'Maria Stubbs—Capability Stubbs they call me. I suppose you are a fresher?'

'Yes,' said Lucy, 'I'm a fresher; I've only just come up. My name is Rae—Lucy Rae.'

'Not a bad name; but you won't have any use for it here. They'll call you Lucifer most likely; they don't call anybody by their right name here.'

Maria Stubbs' room was unlike most Newnham rooms. It was distinctly utilitarian. There was nothing æsthetic about it. The most prominent thing in it was a bookshelf full of books, and there was a cabinet in one corner with a lot of narrow drawers, which Lucy found out after were crammed with specimens. A bright fire was burning in the little tiled grate, and a cloth was spread, and some tea-things were laid on the flap of the bureau, which was let down for the purpose, and there were some cakes in one of the pigeon-holes.

'Take off your hat and sit down,' said Maria, drawing a low chair to the fire; 'there's nothing to hurry for, they won't bring in your things for a long time; they never hurry themselves at Newnham.'

'I don't think I ought to take off my things until I've seen someone,' said Lucy. 'There's Miss Wrayburne I certainly ought to see. Perhaps she doesn't know I'm here.'

The girl laughed—or cackled, rather; there wasn't the least fun in her laugh.

'Perhaps not,' she said, as she busied herself about making the tea; 'and I don't think it would make any difference if she did. You don't think the Dons are running about the college all day long shaking hands with the girls? You'll see Miss Wrayburne at the "High" at dinner, and she'll say "How d'ye do?" and smile—she always smiles—and that's all.'

'I didn't know,' Lucy said humbly. 'I'm only a fresher, you see; I shall know better soon. But it struck me as a very chilling reception.'

Miss Stubbs cackled in her unfeeling way.

'Chilling! that's lovely! You've come to the wrong place if you expect any warmth at Newnham, or sympathy either. It would be nothing better than a big girls' school if we were always "How-d'ye-doing" and shaking hands with each other—we should get to *kissing* soon! Thank goodness there is no spooning here! We are barely civil to each other; and we make a point of ignoring everybody if we meet 'em out-of-doors. I hope you won't, on the strength of this tea, nod to me if you happen to run against me in the street, because I shan't notice you.'

'No,' said Lucy, 'I certainly won't nod to you.' She didn't say it at all humbly, but she drank Miss Stubbs' tea. It was very good tea for Newnham.

# CHAPTER IV
# PAMELA GWATKIN

Lucy saw the Principal, as Miss Stubbs had said, at dinner. She came into the hall rather late, and took her seat at the High table.

It is necessary to spell it with a capital H, as it is distinctly a proper noun, and in Newnham parlance, like the tables in men's colleges where the Dons eat their dinners, it is known as the 'High.'

Miss Wrayburne came in rather late, after the rest were seated, and took her place at the head of the 'High,' and then followed a moment's interval for grace, and then the murmur of tongues began—a low, distinctly female murmur, and occasionally a laugh—a little low laugh. There was a good deal of talk to-day, as everybody had come up fresh, and the atmosphere of the vacation was still about them, and nobody had begun work yet. They would unpack their books by-and-by, and then everything would be changed.

Lucy did not know a soul in the place, except Maria Stubbs, and she sat at another table. She sat quite at the other end of the room, and never once looked Lucy's way, and brushed by her in the corridor as if she had never seen her before.

'She needn't be afraid I shall notice her, the horrid red-haired thing!' Lucy said to herself with quite unnecessary warmth, when Maria looked the other way. 'I wouldn't notice her for the world!'

There were quite half a dozen tables between her and Maria, long narrow tables, with some half-dozen girls at each—girls who ignored everybody else except their own set, and talked across a stranger as if she were a dummy.

They talked across Lucy, and she listened to their talk with a red spot burning on her cheeks and her heart beating. She had not much appetite for the dinner, and she got up from the table with a strange choking sensation that brought the tears smarting to her eyes. She took some comfort in the thought that some day she would talk across a fresher. Her turn would come some day; and while her mind was occupied with this agreeable reflection Miss Wrayburne smiled at her, and said:

'How do you do?'

'How do you do?' may mean a great deal, or it may mean nothing. It didn't mean very much from Miss Wrayburne's lips, and the smile that accompanied it meant less. If it had been a whole smile, or a smile meant entirely for Lucy, there might have been something in it; but it was only the fag-end of a smile that had already been distributed over half a dozen girls.

Lucy accepted it meekly; and with those red spots burning on her cheeks and a choky feeling in her throat she went back to her room—her little desolate, bare room. She felt so utterly miserable and lonely on this wretched first night that she sat down on the side of her bed and had a little weep. Everything was so different to what she had expected; all her castles had been so rudely thrown down.

And then, while she was weeping these foolish tears, she remembered a little curate—a weak-minded young man with red hair; perhaps Miss Stubbs had recalled him—who had once asked her to be his wife. She had refused him indignantly. What girl in her senses would accept a curate with red hair and one hundred and fifty pounds a year? She was not sure, if he had come to her now as she sat in that dismal room, feeling so utterly lonely and miserable, that she would have given him the same answer. She wanted a little love so much; and he loved her in spite of his red hair. She was not so certain, after all, that the higher education of women is quite the best thing—the thing most to be desired in the world. There are other things— she had not thought of them till now, as she sat weeping at the edge of the bed—that make up a woman's life: love, religion, duty, ministering to the wants of others; but love chiefly. She was not sure, after all, if this was not the *summum bonum* of a woman's life.

Lucy was so utterly miserable as she sat there weeping that, if the red-haired curate had come to her at that weak moment, she would have thrown over all her ambitions, she would have given up the higher education altogether, and she would have gone away with him to that poor little moorland cottage, and pinched, and pared, and slaved for him, as dear women before her have pinched and slaved for those they love ever since the world began.

While she was still thinking of the curate, and the tears were dropping into her lap, there was a knock at the door, and someone came in. Lucy started guiltily, and hurriedly wiped her eyes. It was not the red-headed curate. It was a girl—to be more correct, a woman. Everybody is a woman at Newnham. A second-year girl, who had called to see if she could help her to unpack her things and get her room in order.

It wasn't a formal 'call.' Calls at Newnham are usually made after ten p.m., when work is supposed to be over and one is yearning for bed. The second-year girl was a little bit of a thing—smaller than Lucy. A girl who looked as if she had shrunk—as if she had once been round, and plump, and bright-eyed, and soft-cheeked, and red-lipped as a girl ought to be at twenty. She was none of these things now. She was lean and angular; her eyes were dull, her lips were pale, and her cheeks had lost all their youthful roundness and rosiness, if they had ever had any. The roundness had gone into her figure, her back was quite round, her shoulders were bent and stooping, and her chest was narrow and flat like a board.

She had been at Newnham two years, and she was twenty now, and wore glasses, but, alas! not 'sweet and twenty.' She looked exactly like a girl who had used up all her brains.

'I think you have made a mistake,' she said, as she knelt upon the ground unpacking Lucy's books, 'in taking Classics. You should take the Natural Science Tripos. Classics are a thing of the past. They are quite worn out. They will be superseded altogether shortly. Soon—very soon—Latin and Greek will not be compulsory in the examinations; we shall have more useful subjects. Life is so short—so very short' (she was just twenty)—'that we have no time for learning things that will not help us in the rush. Life is getting more of a rush every day, and Science is the only thing that can help us forward. There is no knowing where Science will lead us!'

She clasped her hands, and gasped at the bare thought of it.

'No,' said Lucy, in a low-spirited way.

She hadn't the least interest where Science was going to lead the girl on the floor—it wasn't likely to lead her very far—but she did object to see her pet Classics turned out of the box in that scornful way.

'You will learn all this trash,' the girl continued, opening the pages of Lucy's Euripides and letting the leaves drop through her fingers as if they were not of very much account, 'and you will pore over these rubbishy stories of a quite barbarous age—stories and fables and metamorphoses that, if they were written at the present time, would lay the writer open to a prosecution for perverting the public morals. You will soak your mind with all this nonsense and impurity, and you will think that you have attained culture. Oh, to think how girls waste their lives!'

'I'm sure Classics are ever so much nicer than Natural Science,' Lucy said with some spirit. 'Look at the dreadful subjects you have to study! and to sit side by side with men in lecture-rooms, and listen to lectures on things most women would blush to speak of! Oh, I wouldn't be a Natural Science student for the world!'

The atmosphere of Newnham was beginning to tell. A few hours ago Lucy was as meek as a mouse, and if anyone had slapped her on one cheek she would have been quite ready to offer the other. Now she had plucked up sufficient spirit to defend her choice of a Tripos.

If Newnham doesn't do anything else for a girl, it teaches her to take her own part.

Lucy didn't learn the lesson all at once. It takes a long time to learn, when one has been brought up in the old-fashioned way, to consider other people first and to think of self last. It would never do to practise such a foolish doctrine at a college for women. There is only one person to consider—self, self, self!

Lucy had a great deal to unlearn when she came to Newnham, and a great deal to learn; and she did not learn it all at once. She had always had somebody else to consider first, and now it was ever Number One. Oh, that horrid Number One!

Everybody called upon her in Newe Hall the first week, and some of the girls from the other Halls called later on. The girls at Newe called generally after ten o'clock at night, when she was too sleepy to talk to them, and they went away and voted her 'stupid,' and took no further trouble about her.

Among the girls who called upon Lucy when she was nearly asleep, and went away and voted her stupid, was Pamela Gwatkin, a girl who was much looked up to and worshipped at Newnham. It was no wonder Pamela thought her stupid. She was the leader of the most advanced set in the college, and held opinions that would make one's hair stand on end.

There will be a good many Pamela Gwatkins by-and-by, when there are more Newnhams and the world is ripe for them. They will quite revolutionize society.

They will not be misunderstood like the Greek women of old. Nobody will question their morals because they seek to lead and teach men. Men will be quite willing to be taught by them. It will no longer be a shame for a woman to speak or preach in public. There will be nothing to debar them from taking orders.

Women have proved long ago that they can reach beyond such heights of scholarship as are demanded from a candidate for ordination. But women of Pamela Gwatkin's order will not go into the pulpit—their demands will be even more audacious.

Lucy hadn't any opinions in particular, she was only a fresher; but she was such a poor-spirited creature that she went with the herd and worshipped the very ground that Pamela Gwatkin walked upon.

She hadn't even the excuse of a nodding acquaintance with her after that unlucky call—she only caught glimpses of her at a distant table at Hall, or met her by chance in the library, or ran against her in the streets, coming and going from lectures, when Pamela looked over her head in her superior way and ignored her completely.

She could very well look over Lucy's head, for she stood six feet in her shoes—they had rather high heels. A tall, fair girl, not plump or round by any means, nor rosy-cheeked—she was not a milkmaid; she was an advanced thinker—but lithe, and elastic, and dignified—very dignified.

Lucy thought she had never seen anyone so dignified in her life as Pamela on the night of the first debate of the term at Newnham.

She opened the debate on this particular evening—it happened to be some question of woman's rights which she was always advocating—and she spoke for half an hour without a single pause or hitch.

Some people confess that they cannot bear to hear a woman speak; that when a woman stands up to speak in public it always gives them the sensation of cold water running down their backs. No one who listened to Pamela Gwatkin would have this uncomfortable sensation for a moment. It seemed as if she had been made to stand up in public; as if Nature had intended her for a female orator, and had given her the voice—the clear, penetrating, resonant voice—the quiet, assured manner, the full, free flow of words, without which no woman may attempt to stand on a public platform.

Pamela Gwatkin had all these rare gifts, and she had opinions—very advanced opinions—on every subject under the sun—religion, morals, science, philosophy—nothing came amiss to her. When women are admitted into Parliament she will probably represent an important constituency, perhaps the University.

Lucy, looking down from the gallery above, listened breathlessly, and when the debate was over watched her sailing down the hall in her pale violet gown, with the soft folds of her train gliding noiselessly after her. They didn't rustle and sweep like the frills and furbelows of the other girl, who came *frou-frouing* down the room, pencil in hand, counting the votes. She might have spared her pains; of course, every girl in her senses voted with Pamela.

There was a dance as usual after the debate, and the unique spectacle of fifty female couples spinning round untainted by the arm of man. Pamela Gwatkin danced as well as she spoke, but she didn't put any enthusiasm into it. She took it as the least troublesome way of taking exercise, but she didn't put any spirit into it. She didn't smile once all the evening, except in a weary, disdainful way when her partner broke down or fell out of the ring. She never broke down or fell out herself, and when she had tired out one girl she took up another. Lucy remarked that she always chose small girls—the smallest girls she could find—and that they were invariably 'gentlemen.' Lucy was wondering how ever they could drag her round, when, to her consternation, Pamela stopped in front of her.

She had worn out all the other small girls in the room, and she had to fall back upon Lucy. The silly little thing stood up in quite a flutter. If a Royal Highness had asked her to dance she could not have been more flattered. Of course, she would take 'gentleman'! She told the most outrageous fibs, and said she preferred being 'gentleman;' she always chose it when she had the chance.

After she had dragged Pamela round until she was fit to faint, and had ascertained how hard her whalebones were, and how regular her breathing, and that her favourite perfume was heliotrope, and that dancing with a goddess whose chin was on a level with the top of her head was not all pure bliss, she had her reward.

Annabel Crewe, the Natural Science girl, asked her to 'cocoa' after the dancing was over, and here she met Pamela. It was Lucy's first experience of a Newnham 'cocoa.' There was quite a spread on Annabel Crewe's little writing-table—sweets and cakes and fruit, and cups brimming over with the nectar of Newnham.

Pamela Gwatkin came in last; there was a crowd of girls in the room when she came in, filling it quite up, and occupying all the chairs and the ottoman and both sides of the bed. There was an art covering thrown over the bed embroidered with dragons, and a cushion with an impossible monster with a flaming tail; nobody but a Newnham girl would have dreamed it was a bed.

Lucy was occupying a low cushiony-chair—the nicest chair in the room—and she got up directly Pamela came in and gave it up to her. She accepted it in her superior way, and flopped down into it as if it were in the order of things for everyone to make place for her. Then that wretched little sycophant, Lucy, waited upon her in her servile way, as if she were nothing short of a Royal Princess. She brought her her cocoa, and sweets, and cakes, and fruit. She positively snatched them from the other girls to offer them to Pamela, and be snubbed for her pains. She hadn't the spirit of a mouse.

Everybody was talking at once, and there was such a clatter of tongues that Lucy couldn't have heard the goddess speak if she had deigned to speak to her. She did deign just before the party broke up.

Lucy hadn't anywhere to sit, and she was tired out with dragging Pamela round, and she had found an idiotic three-legged milking-stool, and she was trying to sit upon it. It was an objectionable stool; in the first place, it had been painted with yellow buttercups, and varnished before the paint was dry. It was not dry yet, and it stuck to Lucy's black gown and left a proof impression of the buttercups on the back. In the second place, the legs hadn't been stuck in firmly, and it wobbled under her weight and threatened to collapse every moment. Lucy sat in fear and trembling, trying to look as if she were quite comfortable and used to wobbling, and while she sat the goddess spoke:

'I have a brother at St. Benedict's,' she said; 'I dare say you know him; he is in his third year.'

Lucy murmured that she hadn't that pleasure; she didn't know any undergraduates.

'No, I suppose not,' Pamela said wearily—she generally spoke wearily, as if commonplace subjects were beneath her. 'They are an uninteresting class; only Eric is so quixotic; he does such absurd things that I should not have thought he could have been anywhere long without being known and laughed at.'

'Really!' said Lucy, in rather a shocked voice; she didn't know what else to say.

'It was one of his absurdities to come up here as an undergraduate. He had qualified—fully qualified—for another profession. He was a doctor, and when he had passed all his examinations, after seven years' work, he threw it all up. He found out that he had missed his right vocation. He had some absurd notion that he was specially called for the Church—that the Church couldn't do without him—and so he has come up here.'

Pamela spoke scornfully, with her thin upper lip curling, and just a suspicion of pink in her face—her beautiful worn, weary face.

'Perhaps he has done right,' said Lucy. 'A man ought never to go into the Church unless he feels that he is called. Papa might have been Senior

Wrangler, but he felt his vocation was the Church. He gave up everything for it, and——' 'And mamma' she was going to say, but she looked at Pamela and stopped short.

'It would be all very well if the Church were going to last,' she said wearily; 'but it isn't. Everybody knows that it isn't. Nobody but women and children believe in it now. Its methods are all exploded; its teaching is preposterous; it has had its day, like other beliefs, and now a new day is dawning. Oh, it was ridiculous of Eric to go into the Church just as it was falling to pieces!'

Lucy was past expressing an opinion. The milking-stool had collapsed. The three idiotic legs had all gone different ways; it had fallen quite to pieces, like the Church was going to, and Lucy was seated on the floor.

# CHAPTER V
# AFTER CHAPEL

The day succeeding the debate was Sunday, and Lucy went over to St. Benedict's to morning chapel.

She was so glad to go. It was quite a relief to get outside Newnham and shake from her skirts the atmosphere of so much learning. It was a distinct relief to take her place in the stalls of St. Benedict's and look down upon the men who took life so much more easily.

She was only just in time for the college chapel. The bell was going as she crossed the court, and the men were hurrying in in their white surplices. They were all smiling and debonair. There wasn't a single cloud on the brow of one of them, except the cloud of last night's tobacco. They were lusty and strong and fresh-coloured, and some of them had frames like giants; and they came across the court with a swinging stride, and health and life and vigour in every movement. Men take things so much more easily than women.

The choir and the Master came in directly after Lucy had taken her seat. The Master looked across his wife and Mary, who sat between them, and nodded to Lucy.

'Very glad to see you, my dear,' he said in quite an audible voice.

It was a longer service than usual at St. Benedict's on Sunday mornings. The Master read the Litany, and he took a long time in reading it, and Lucy had plenty of opportunity of looking among the men for Pamela Gwatkin's brother.

He was a twin brother, she had learned from Annabel Crewe, who knew all about Pamela, and therefore he ought to be exactly like her. Tall and fair and thin-lipped, with clear, steady eyes—blue ought to be the colour, or gray, she was not sure which; but she could not mistake the profile. There could be no doubt about that clear-cut face, without an ounce of superfluous flesh upon it.

Lucy looked at the men eagerly one after the other; she looked at every man in the chapel. The Senior Tutor from his stall on the other side saw her looking down at the men. She didn't look at him, and he wondered at the change in her. Her eyes were not wont to rove over the faces of the men sitting below in that eager way; they might have all been sticks and stones for the notice Lucy had hitherto vouchsafed them.

Was this the outcome of a week at Newnham? Had she seen so much—so very, very much—of women in her new developments that she was thirsting for the sight of man?

Cousin Mary saw her looking down at the undergraduates in the seat below, too, and sighed. She remembered the time when she used to look across the benches. She had seen so many generations of undergraduates come and go in fifteen years. She may have looked more than once in all that time to see if among them there was that one face that was to be her beacon through life; she had ceased to look for it now.

Lucy had decided before she left the chapel that the man in the third row near the top was Pamela's brother. A tall man with a thin, fair, fresh-coloured face and firm lips—a capable face, a face quite worthy of the brother of Pamela Gwatkin.

Lucy watched the men file out of chapel, and the man in the last seat of the last row naturally came out last. She refused to go into the lodge with Mary. She let the old Master and his wife toddle off down the cloisters together, and she stood holding Mary back and begging her to wait 'just a minute.'

The man in the back seat came out at last and took off his cap to the Master's nieces as he passed.

'There!' said Lucy breathlessly, 'this is the man I waited for. Is he Eric Gwatkin?'

'Eric Gwatkin!' Mary repeated impatiently; she objected to being kept standing in the court watching the men come out of chapel; she could see them every day—twice a day if she liked—and she had seen them for fifteen years. 'Eric Gwatkin?' she repeated. 'The man who has just come out is Wyatt Edgell, the best man of the year. He will take a very high place in the Tripos—perhaps the highest—and Eric Gwatkin is only a Poll man. He is taking the theological Special, I believe, and I dare say he will be plucked.'

'Oh, I am sure there is some mistake!' Lucy said hotly; 'Pamela's brother never could be plucked. She is awfully clever, and—and he is a twin.'

Cousin Mary didn't take the least interest in Pamela's brother; even the fact of his being a twin didn't move her. She went into the lodge and looked after the table that was spread for lunch. She altered the arrangement of the flowers, and put some finishing touches to it, and Lucy stood beside the window that overlooked the court watching her.

She couldn't help pitying Mary for being interested in such small things, for being taken up with such petty cares. She had lived in the midst of culture for fifteen years, and yet she could potter about that dinner-table and be absorbed in the arrangement of the flowers.

'I am very glad to see you, my dear,' the old Master said to Lucy when she had dutifully kissed him and whispered to her aunt how well he was looking—the sure key to that dear, kind, simple heart was to tell her how well the Master was looking. It would be a sad day when those welcome words could no longer be said.

'And how is the Greek getting on, my dear? Who would have thought of my brother Dick's daughter learning Greek? She didn't get the taste for it from her father, for he was no scholar. He was good only for his own work, none better. There was not a man in the parish who could drive a straighter furrow than my brother Dick, and his wife was famous for her poultry. I remember her carrying her butter and eggs to market. She had the corner stall in the old butter market, my dear. I mind the very spot.'

'It was my grandmother, or great-grandmother, rather,' said Lucy, feebly trying to set him right. 'Mamma never kept a stall in the butter market.'

'Never mind which it was,' said the Senior Tutor, who had just come in, and was shaking hands with Lucy; 'a generation or two doesn't matter.'

It didn't matter to him, who knew all the homely details of the Master's humble history; but suppose he were to go maundering about that stall in the butter market to Pamela Gwatkin, it would be all over Newnham that it was Lucy's mother, and that Lucy herself used to milk the cows. With such a pedigree there was no excuse for her tumbling off a milking-stool.

If Lucy hadn't been so full of her own concerns that she had no eyes for others, she would have seen the reason for Cousin Mary's anxiety about the dinner-table. The Senior Tutor was coming to dinner.

The lunch, or rather the dinner—for it was a real dinner; except on state occasions, the old Master dined in the middle of the day—was spread in the dining-room of the lodge—an old, old room panelled up to the ceiling with dark oak, with a delightful carved frieze running round the top, and a big oriel window with diamond panes and stained glass coats-of-arms of the old Masters who had occupied the lodge since it was first built, centuries ago.

There were portraits of some of them in their scarlet gowns on the walls, looking down upon them as they sat at meat. It was a ghostly company, so many old Masters, and soon there would be another to hang among them. He was painted already, and hanging in the gallery outside; he would come in here soon, and take his place, not at the table, but on the walls with the rest.

Perhaps the Senior Tutor was thinking of that not far-off time as he lay back in his chair glancing up at the dingy old walls that wanted beeswaxing dreadfully. There would be plenty for him to do when his time came. There had been nothing done here for years. He would have to go right through the house; he hardly knew where he should begin.

And then Lucy broke in upon his pleasant reverie, and asked him about Eric Gwatkin.

'Gwatkin?' said the Tutor absently. He was just considering whether he should have the oak varnished or beeswaxed. 'Ye—e—s; he's going in for his Special, but I don't think he'll get through.'

'Only his Special!' Lucy hadn't got through her Little-go yet, but she regarded the Special from the Newnham standpoint. No woman has ever yet descended so low as a Special. 'His sister is one of the cleverest girls at Newnham. She has already taken a first in one Tripos, and now she is working for another. She is sure to take a double-first. He is her twin brother, and I'm sure she expects great things of him.'

'Then I'm very sorry for Miss Gwatkin,' the Tutor said with a laugh. 'If he gets through it's as much as he will do.'

He declined to have anything more to say about Pamela's unpromising brother; and he talked to Lucy until the ladies left the table about her life at Newnham, and the progress she was making with her work.

The old Master did not sit long over his wine; it had come to one glass now after dinner—one glass of that old, old wine that had already lain a dozen years in the darkness of the college cellar when he had come up a raw scholar to St. Benedict's. It did him quite as much good as a dozen glasses of a less generous vintage. It brought a warm flush into his wrinkled cheeks, and a light into his dim eyes, and stirred the slow blood circling round his heart, and it sent him to sleep to dream again of the old time, and to win afresh the laurels of his youth. While the Master sat nodding in his big chair on one side of the wide fireplace, where a fire was still burning, and his faithful partner sat nodding on the other side, Lucy slipped out of the room.

She was only going to the old study to find some books, but she had to pass through the picture-gallery to reach it. The gallery of the lodge of St.

Benedict's was very much like the galleries of most college lodges, only it was narrower—a long, low, narrow old room extending the length of one side of the cloistered court. It had been built when the cloisters beneath had been built, and it had suffered few changes since. The walls were panelled to the ceiling with oak, and it was lighted with deep, old-fashioned bay-windows; not particularly well lighted, as the diamond panes were darkened with painted arms of founders and benefactors, and old, dead and forgotten Fellows. The walls of the long gallery were hung with portraits from end to end. They began in the right-hand corner by the door in the fourteenth century—flat, angular, awful presentments of men and women whose names are household words in Cambridge, and they went on and on until it seemed that they would never cease. The walls were so full that it would be difficult to find room for another Fellow.

Lucy paused on her way to the study, and looked round with quite a new feeling on these old painted faces. They represented something to her to-day that they had not represented before.

She began dimly to understand what had made Cambridge the power it is in the land. It was these still faces looking down from the walls who had built up this great Cambridge. It was the men, after all, the patient men of old, whose toil had accomplished so much; and now the women were entering into their labours.

There were not many portraits at Newnham; it was only in its infancy. There would be plenty by-and-by. Lucy ran over in her mind the women whose portraits would hang upon those white walls between the windows. She could not in that brief retrospect think of any who were doing such great work that they would earn that distinction, only Pamela Gwatkin. She was sure Pamela would one day hang on the walls. She would be an old woman then, most likely, a lean, wrinkled, hard-visaged old woman, with gray hair and spectacles, and she would have a big book beside her—a book she had written or explained—and she would wear—what would she wear?

She would have gone quite bald by that time, like the old Fellows on the walls; her head would be bald and shining. She would wear it covered, of course, with—with a scholar's cap, with a long tassel depending over her nose, or a velvet Doctor's cap, which would be more becoming, and she would wear a scarlet Doctor's gown and hood. The picture would look lovely on the white walls of Newnham.

Lucy had just settled to her satisfaction how Pamela Gwatkin was to be handed down by a future Herkomer to another generation, when the Senior Tutor entered the gallery.

He, too, had been thinking. He hadn't been paying any attention to what Mary Rae had been talking about while the Master took his after-dinner nap; his thoughts were with Lucy in the gallery. He had watched her narrowly at dinner, and he had detected a change in her. He was used to watching men, and now he had begun to watch women. He remarked that her eyes were no longer soft; they were hard and eager, and had a hunted look in them. He knew the look; he had seen it in boys come up fresh from school—not brilliant boys from the sixth form of big public schools, but frank, fresh-faced fellows who had come up from country parsonages. He had seen the look on their faces when the work was new to them and the strain had begun to tell upon them. They lost it after a term or two when they bossed their lectures, and drifted away with the stream, or broke down, and went back to the country parsonages, and never came up again.

He had seen this hunted look on boys' faces, but he had never seen it on a girl's face before. He wasn't sure if it wouldn't be well to take Lucy away before she broke down. She would never want the mathematics she was getting up with such labour for the Little-go; she would be able to add up the butcher's book quite as well without. As the future mistress of the lodge—it had really come to that; he had ceased to think about Mary, and he had almost unconsciously put Lucy in her place—he would have liked her to have the prestige of Newnham, and, considering her humble antecedents, it was quite as well that she should win her spurs. She had pluck enough, if her strength would only hold out. She was a brave little thing; he had never seen a girl so brave. The Little-go examinations would soon be over, and then, if the result was satisfactory, he would speak. She would have quite culture enough after the Little-go—quite enough to condone even the stall in the butter market.

'I think you had better let me coach you for the exam.,' he said, as they talked about her mathematics; 'for the Additionals, at any rate, you'll find the dynamics and the statics rather stiff.'

'Ye—es,' Lucy said with a sigh; 'they are dreadfully stiff.'

'When will you come to me? Will you come here, or shall I come up to Newnham?'

'Oh no, no! It would never do to come to Newnham!'

Lucy turned quite pale at the suggestion.

'You have male lecturers,' said the college Don with a laugh. 'The difference would be that I should only be lecturing one girl instead of six.'

'I'm sure it wouldn't do; I'm sure Miss Wrayburne would object. I would rather, if you don't mind, come to you,' Lucy said meekly.

'Come, by all means. You had better come to my rooms; there will be less interruption than at the lodge. I can give you four hours a week, but it must be in the afternoon. When will you begin?'

Lucy was quite ready to begin at once. She settled to go to the Tutor's rooms the very next day. She didn't even think of consulting Cousin Mary about the arrangement, or the Master, or the Master's wife. She had already made a distinct advance; she had decided for herself; she had engaged a University coach, and arranged to spend four hours a week alone with him in his college rooms. The woman of the future could not do more.

# CHAPTER VI
# BEHIND THE SCREEN

Lucy went to her coach the next day. She ought to have known her way about a college staircase by this time, but she had never yet penetrated beyond the outer courts. She had never ventured up those mysterious stairways sacred to gyps, bed-makers and gownsmen.

A great many gownsmen must have climbed the stairs that led to Mr. Colville's rooms before her; they had left their marks here, if they had left them nowhere else in the annals of the University. Mr. Colville's rooms were in the oldest part of the college, and his staircase was as narrow and steep and dark as any lover of mediæval architecture could desire.

It was so dark that when Lucy reached the first landing she didn't see where to go; there was a passage in front of her and doors on either side. Instead of looking at the names painted over the doors, she went down the passage and knocked at the door at the end.

There are several ways of knocking at a door, but there is only one way of knocking at a college door if one expects to be heard. A timid rap with the knuckles is wasted effort; the knob of an umbrella, or the handle of a walking-stick, or any other form of bludgeon one happens to have at hand, is more effective; or a succession of well-delivered blows with a fist, or the body falling heavily against the door, have been known to attract the attention of persons within the room; but Lucy had recourse to none of these devices. She knocked feebly with her gloved hand on the door and waited. She was sure it was the right landing. She had read the directions painted on the door-post at the foot of the staircase:

First Floor—Mr. Colville.

She knocked again presently; and then, as nobody answered, she went in. The Senior Tutor was expecting her; it was surely right to go in. She thought she heard voices as she opened the door—at least a voice, a voice that had a familiar ring in it; she heard it clearer when she opened the first door; there was an outer oak, as usual to a college room. Lucy opened both doors and went in. She went quite into the room, and closed the door—there was a screen before the door—before she saw the occupants of the room.

What she saw didn't exactly make her hair stand on end, but she gave a little cry. She couldn't help crying out. On the couch behind the screen a man was lying, with the blood flowing from a wound in his throat, and on his knees beside him was a man praying.

The man who was praying stopped and looked up at the sound of that startled cry, and saw Lucy standing in the middle of the floor. He got up from his knees, and with a gesture of silence went behind the screen and fastened the two doors.

'I am glad you are come,' he said, going back to Lucy. 'I did not know the doors were open. You must be sure to keep them fastened. We don't want the authorities to know of this, and the Senior Tutor has the next rooms. You must be sure not to let him suspect anything. If you can do what is necessary for Edgell by day, I will sit up with him at night. It is not a bad wound; I don't think it is at all serious.'

Lucy stood frightened and speechless. What did the man mean? Did he take her for a nurse?

'I am afraid there is some mistake,' she said in a low voice; she couldn't keep from shaking. 'I—I thought this was Mr. Colville's room.'

Then a light seemed to break in upon the man, and he looked at Lucy with a quick, startled glance.

'Oh!' he said, 'I thought you were the nurse. I beg your pardon. There— there has been an accident here; our friend has not been quite himself—he has been over-working—and—and this has happened. Thank God it is no worse! It might have been fatal; a mere hair's breadth and it would have been fatal. We are anxious to keep it from the authorities. It would be very serious for him if it were known. It would ruin him for life. May we ask you to keep the chance knowledge of this most deplorable occurrence secret?'

What could Lucy say? Clearly it was her duty as the Master's niece to go straight to the lodge and acquaint him with the state of affairs. It was her duty to summon Mr. Colville without a moment's loss of time; he was only separated from the scene of this tragedy by a narrow passage.

Of course, the man lying bleeding there ought to have a doctor and a nurse, and his friends should be telegraphed for, and the whole college ought to be thrown into a commotion. Suppose the man were to die, what would her feelings be if she were *particeps criminis* in this dreadful secret?

All these things flashed through Lucy's mind as she stood there looking at the man on the couch. She knew him now; it was the man who had taken his hat off to her as he came out of chapel.

It was the man that Cousin Mary said was going to take a very high place in the Tripos, perhaps the highest. It was Wyatt Edgell.

She made up her mind in a moment.

'Yes,' she said, 'I will keep your secret. But I cannot go away from here and leave you like this. There is something I can do. I am used to nursing and sickness; tell me what I can do.'

She had torn off her gloves and thrown down her books, and was kneeling beside the couch where the man lay, wiping away the blood that was trickling beneath the bandage, and dropping down over his chest.

There was so much she could do that a woman could best do, and the man with his hand on the wrist of the patient stood by and watched her while she did it.

'You know something about medicine?' she said.

'I have been a doctor. I have spent seven years in acquiring a knowledge of surgery—seven years out of my life—but it has not been wasted if I have been the means of saving him;' and he nodded towards the bed.

'And you think you have saved him?'

Where had she heard this man's voice before, and where had she seen his eyes? She was asking herself this question as she was speaking to him.

'Yes, I think he is saved. He will do very well with careful nursing. One of the men has a sister at Addenbroke's, and he has gone to fetch her. I thought she had come when I saw you standing there. She will certainly be here presently. I don't think we need detain you.'

'I shall not go till she comes,' Lucy said with such decision that she quite frightened herself. 'I shall certainly stay here as long as I can be of any use.'

She had been of a good deal of use already. She had removed all traces of the dreadful deed; she had washed up every stain that could be washed away, and she had covered up the rest. She had fetched a pillow and some coverings from the adjoining room, and straightened the couch, and anyone coming into the room and seeing the man lying there with a white handkerchief over his throat, and the quilt drawn up over his chest, would not have dreamed of the ghastly sight beneath.

He looked as he lay there as if he had broken down in the middle of his work, and had thrown himself down there in a sudden attack of faintness. His face was dreadfully white, as white as the coverlet, and he was breathing hard, and there was a strange faint odour Lucy noticed as she bent over him. He was not sensible, but once he opened his eyes and looked at her with a strange, far-away look in them that haunted her for days.

They were beautiful eyes, tender and dreamy as a woman's, with a depth in them Lucy had never seen in any eyes before. But then she had not been accustomed to look into young men's eyes. She could not remember bending over a man before and seeing herself reflected in his eyes.

Perhaps it was the novelty of the situation that moved her. Having done all, everything she could do, she settled herself down in a chair by the head of the bed and began to weep.

The man was nothing to her, she had never heard his name till yesterday, and here she was sitting by his side weeping for him as if she had known him all her life.

The man who stood by let her tears fall unchecked.

'I don't think you will disturb him,' he said with a smile; 'I have given him an anodyne. Nobody could tell what he would do if he were left to himself, so I have made things sure by quieting him for a time. Pray have your cry out if it does you any good.'

He evidently knew something of girls. There is nothing like a little weep for soothing the nerves.

While Lucy was availing herself of her woman's privilege, he turned down the coverlet and examined the bandages; the blood was trickling down beneath them, thick and black where it had congealed, and a paler streak behind.

'It's broken out again,' he said quietly. 'I think there must be a stitch. Can you help me?'

If Lucy had been told an hour ago that she could have stood by and assisted as the man sewed up that gaping wound, and never by word or look betrayed faintness or alarm, she would not have believed it.

It was the little weep that did it.

'I think it will do now,' said the man, drawing up the coverlet over his work. 'There is only one thing we can do more for the poor fellow, and that is commit him to God. Will you kneel down beside him while we ask His blessing on the means that we have used? Remember, when two or three are gathered together—we are two, and—and I am sure his mother is here with us.'

Lucy knelt down beside the couch while the man prayed aloud.

He talked to God as he knelt there as one who knew Him as a Friend of old. He made no preamble in entering this solemn Presence Chamber, but went straight up to the throne with his petition, and laid the poor, blind, suffering soul at the foot of the Cross.

Lucy had been brought up in the bosom of the Church; she had heard prayers read every morning and evening of her life, and she had never missed being in her place on Sundays. She had heard her father read the prayers hundreds of times, and she had heard, oh, so many sermons, but she had never heard a man pray like this.

It was heart speaking to heart; it was the spirit of man speaking to the Spirit of God.

While he was still speaking the door, or doors, rather, opened, and someone came in. He did not stop or get up from his knees, but went on wrestling for the blessing that he sought.

Lucy felt dreadfully guilty kneeling there. She heard the door open, and people—distinctly people—come in; and she had an awful overwhelming sense of guiltiness, as if she had been consenting to a murder. She was afraid to get up; she expected to see the Senior Tutor standing there and her cousin Mary. She didn't at all know why she expected Mary.

She was almost afraid to look up when she rose from her knees, and she felt herself shaking all over. But it was not Mary, and it was not the Tutor. It was a man that Lucy had often seen in the courts below, and he had a girl in a nurse's dress with him.

He looked over to Lucy in some alarm, and took off his cap.

'It's all right,' said the other. 'You didn't lock the door after you, old man, when you went out, and this lady found her way in—at least, God showed her the way in. If she hadn't come at the right moment it would have gone hard with our friend here. I am glad you have brought your sister. And now,' he said, turning to Lucy, 'we need not detain you any longer. This lady will stay with us, I hope, till late; and I shall sit up with him to-night. To-morrow, I hope, the worst will be over.'

'I hope so,' Lucy said with a sob she couldn't choke down—she hadn't the heart to say any more.

'I am sure you will respect our secret,' the man said, as Lucy was drawing on her gloves.

She didn't answer him; she only looked at him, and she saw the blood flush up under his skin. She remembered somebody else's cheeks she had seen flush in the same way—not a man's.

'I beg your pardon,' he said humbly.

Lucy was so angry with him for doubting her that she did not see his proffered hand; she drew her gloves on hurriedly, and picked up her books and went out into the passage, but she beckoned the nurse to follow her.

'I don't think the man's going to get better,' she said in a hurried whisper. 'It's like consenting to a murder to let him lie there and die; but *I* am not going to tell. I think his mother ought to know. I think someone ought to write and tell her that he is ill—dying!'

The nurse shook her head.

'It would kill her!' she said. 'She has such faith in her son—her beautiful son! He is such a noble, splendid fellow! Oh, it is a dreadful pity!'

'Why did he do it?'

'Why? Oh, don't you know?'

'No——'

The door of the room opened as they were speaking, and the nurse's brother beckoned her to come in.

'Come to me to-morrow morning at Addenbroke's,' she said. 'Ask for Nurse Brannan;' and then she went into the room and shut the door.

Lucy crept guiltily down the stairs. She quite shivered as she passed the Tutor's door: she would not have encountered him for the world. She didn't feel safe until she had got outside the college gate, and then she ran all the way back to Newnham.

# CHAPTER VII
# LUCY'S SECRET

Lucy felt dreadfully guilty all through that wretched evening. If she had assisted in a murder she couldn't have felt worse.

She had no appetite for dinner, and when she went back to her room, what was still more unusual, she had no appetite for her work. A Newnham girl is a gourmand where work is concerned; she may leave her meals untasted, but that terrible craving within creates an appetite that is akin to ravenous where work is concerned. When that craving ceases she goes down—or breaks down.

It had ceased quite suddenly with Lucy; she hated the very thought of work; she loathed with an unutterable loathing the sight of those mathematical books she had brought back from St. Benedict's. She shrank from them with a dreadful sense of faintness and sickness when she attempted to open them. They smelt of blood, or else she fancied they did.

The air was full of fancies. It was a stormy night, and the wind was wailing round her corner of the building, and every now and then a sharp blast of driving rain would strike upon her window. She heard the rain distinctly dropping down the pane like tears, and she fancied—oh, it was a dreadful fancy!—that it was drops of blood.

She bore it in that lonely room as long as she could, and then she got up and went out into the passage. The lights were out, and the place was quite still; everybody had gone to bed. Dark and deserted as the corridor was, it was not so lonely as her own room. There were girls sleeping behind every one of those closed doors. She heard them—for the ventilators of most were open—breathing audibly, and some were moaning in their sleep.

Lucy walked up and down the long corridor; her feet were bare, and she had thrown nothing over her shoulders. Cousin Mary would have scolded her dreadfully if she had seen her, with her white garments trailing on the stone floor.

She never thought of the draughts or the cold stones; she only thought of getting away from that everlasting drip, drip of the window-pane, that brought the scene of the afternoon so vividly before her. She was nervous and overwrought, and she was burdened with a secret she ought never to have bound herself to keep.

Wild horses shouldn't tear it from her, she told herself, as she paced up and down that draughty passage. Whatever happened, she would be true to her word. It would be hard if a girl couldn't be trusted as well as a man. What was the use of coming to Newnham if gossip and emptiness—the habits of the slave—still had dominion over her?

It was all very fine and high-sounding; but she would have given the world to have told somebody, to have eased her overburdened mind and poured out the dreadful story on some soft feminine, sympathetic bosom.

And then, while she was telling herself all these fine things, and repeating Lord Tennyson's nice verses about that open fountain that was to wash away all those silly human things and make woman perfect—quite perfect—a strange thing happened.

She heard the voice of the man praying. He was praying now; she heard him quite distinctly, but she could not catch the words. She was quite sure it was the voice; it had sunk down so deep into her ears that she could never forget it. Lucy paused in the darkness and listened. The voice came from a room at the door of which she was standing. She had no idea, in the darkness, whose room it was; she was only sure—quite sure—of the voice.

An overpowering desire to see the speaker—perhaps to get her release— seized her, and she opened the door of the room.

There was no man there praying; there was only a girl sitting reading by the light of a shaded lamp, and she was reading aloud. It was Pamela Gwatkin, and she was reading a Greek play.

Lucy went a few paces into the room and stood there as if spellbound, listening to the girlish voice, in low solemn accents, mouthing the rhythmic Greek. She didn't read it as if it were Wordsworth, or Cowper, or Keats, or even Tennyson; she mouthed it; and the noble words, falling in noble cadence, brought back the voice of the man wrestling with God for his friend.

Pamela heard the door open, and she looked up. She didn't divide the shuddering night with a shrill-edged shriek, and bring all Newnham about her, as she might have done at the sight of the white-robed figure standing in the doorway. She thought it was a girl walking in her sleep, and she got up softly and went towards her.

For a moment, as she came forward, she saw the figure swaying in the doorway, and as she came nearer Lucy tottered forward with her arms outstretched like one walking in a dream, and fell upon her bosom—literally fell, with her clinging arms around her, and her head pillowed on Pamela's bosom.

'Oh, it is Eric Gwatkin!' she sobbed, 'it is Eric Gwatkin!'

Pamela got her over to the couch—it was a bed now, not a couch; the serge rug had been removed, and a snowy coverlet was in its place, and a real pillow, not a sham roundabout bolster covered with an embroidered dragon.

Pamela Gwatkin laid the girl down on her own bed and covered her up. She was shaking dreadfully, and her hands and feet were like ice, and she was sobbing hysterically.

When Pamela had covered her up, she shut the door of the room; it was no good making a scene and arousing everybody, because a girl—a little weak-minded fresher—had broken down under the strain and got hysterical. All girls get hysterical at times, only the stronger ones lock the door and wrestle with the enemy in secret.

'Oh, Eric Gwatkin!' moaned the girl on the bed. 'I can't keep it any longer; I must tell!'

'What have you got to do with Eric Gwatkin?' Pamela asked severely. 'I am sure he is nothing to you; he is never likely to be anything to anybody.'

'Oh yes, he is! He is everything to—to Wyatt Edgell. He has saved his life. Oh, you don't know what he is to him!'

'Saved his life? What are you talking about? What has Wyatt Edgell got to do with you, and with Eric?'

'*He sewed it up*—the wound—the dreadful gaping wound!'

Lucy covered her eyes with her hands to shut out the dreadful sight, and she was trembling so dreadfully that the bed shook with her. Clearly the girl was in a fever, and her mind was wandering. The name of Wyatt Edgell was familiar to Pamela; it was familiar to everybody in Cambridge. He was the coming Senior Wrangler. What could Eric have to do with him— poor Eric, who was grinding for his 'Special'?

'What wound?' said Pamela impatiently; 'and who sewed it up?'

'Eric sewed it up, and I helped him. I drew the edges together, while he put the needle in the quivering flesh. Oh, it was horrible!'

Lucy sank back on the couch, and her lips grew pale, and her cheeks gray, and Pamela thought she was going to faint. She hadn't got anything but eau-de-Cologne to give her—not a nip of brandy for the world; not even a pocket flask is allowed at Newnham. She went to the water-jug and poured out some water in a basin, and dabbed it over the girl's face and hands, and made her own bed streaming. Perhaps there was something in the girl's story, after all! She couldn't have dreamed these hideous details.

'Where was the wound? how had he hurt himself?' she asked presently.

'He had cut his throat.'

Pamela let the basin of water she was holding fall on the floor. She didn't scream as any less well-regulated mind would have done, but she let the basin slip out of her hands, and the water made a dreadful mess on the floor.

'Cut his throat?' she repeated faintly—she was nearly as white as Lucy—'and Eric——'

'Eric sewed it up.'

'Is—is he dead?'

She asked the question hoarsely, in a voice Lucy couldn't have recognised for Pamela's, but she was past noticing voices.

'No—o; Eric has asked God to give him back his life, that he may begin it afresh.'

'What use is that?' said Pamela bitterly.

'I am sure God heard him—we were praying for him when the nurse came in. He was asking that the nurse might be sent quickly, and she came while the words were on his lips.'

'Of course the nurse would be sent; you can get a nurse at any moment from Addenbroke's without praying for one.'

'Oh, you don't understand!' Lucy moaned; 'you don't know the worst. It had to be done secretly: no one must know. It would ruin him for life if it were known.'

'You don't mean that they haven't told anyone? that they are trying to hush it up, and not let the tutors know?'

Lucy moaned.

'Oh, what folly is this! I am sure Eric is at the bottom of it.'

'Yes; it was Eric made me promise I wouldn't tell, and I have told you,' Lucy murmured helplessly.

'Of course you have told me. Having told me so much, you must tell me all—you must keep nothing back.'

And so Lucy sat up in the bed with her arms round Pamela—she couldn't have told her without having something to cling to—and told her her wretched little story, and how she had pledged herself to keep this young man's secret.

'What do you think I ought to do?' she asked weakly, when the recital was finished.

'Do?' said Pamela, but she didn't answer the girl's question. She disengaged herself from her clinging arms, and she paced up and down the room, her feet dabbling in the water on the floor. She stopped presently in her walk, her chin up, and her face set with the light of a high resolve upon it towards the light that was breaking in at the east window; she might have been reciting that Greek play. 'Do?' she repeated, and her face was hard and cold and tired. The old weary look had come back to it—no wonder; it was three o'clock in the morning. 'Do? Why, go to bed, of course!'

She refused to say another word about Lucy's secret. She helped her back to her room, and put her to bed, and tucked her in, and drew back the curtains, that the light of the new day might drive away the ghosts of the night.

Pamela did all this without speaking a word; but when she got to the door of Lucy's room she stopped and looked back. She could see from the tremulous motion of the clothes that the girl was weeping, and she went over to the bed and put her cool lips to Lucy's forehead.

'Good-night, dear!' she said softly. 'I think you have behaved beautifully!'

# CHAPTER VIII
# WATTLES

As soon as she could get away from Newnham the next morning, Lucy went to Addenbroke's to see Nurse Brannan. She couldn't get away very early; there was a mathematical lecture at nine o'clock that wasn't over till eleven, and she had to plod, plod through those weary diagrams while her mind was far away. Oh, how she hated those problems and riders, and all the dreary, dreary round! She made one or two futile little diagrams on her paper, and then she rubbed them out again, and sat staring at the blackboard, and watching the perplexing white lines come and go while her mind was far away. She was calculating what would happen if the man had died in the night.

'What would they do with the body? Would Eric Gwatkin expect her to keep the secret, and assist, perhaps, at some mysterious obsequies?' It was with a distinct feeling of relief she saw the duster sweep over the blackboard and wipe all those cabalistic characters away. It was like wiping out the record of her guilt.

Lucy shook off the dust and gloom of the lecture-room and ran off to Addenbroke's. She really could run a good part of the way. She went across the Fens, as less frequented, and giving her space to breathe and think. It was such a blue day, and the fresh green of the year was over the low-lying fields, and the chestnut-tree by the bridge was budding, and the pollard willows that marked the winding course of the river were sallow-gray in the sunshine, and the daisies were in bloom. Lucy walked over quite a carpet of flowers; she crushed the little tender pink buds remorselessly under her feet in her hurry to get to Addenbroke's.

She had never been to the hospital before, and she was rather afraid to go in when she got there. There were a lot of people coming out with newly-bandaged limbs and white faces, and some children were carried in in their mothers' arms. There were people of all ages, men and women, and little children all with that sad patience on their faces which is born of suffering. Lucy was so sorry for the people. She had no idea her heart was still tender; she had rather prided herself on its growing cold and hard like

Maria Stubbs and the rest of the Stoics of Newnham. There was a tired-looking woman coming up the path with a puny little creature in her arms, with, oh! such a white, white face. Its eyes were open, and it was smiling a wan little smile up into the mother's face, and she was crooning over it; she was a poor, weakly thing, and she carried it as if even its light weight were too much for her. Lucy turned to look after the sickly mother and the sickly child, and she noticed the child's arm—a lean, puny little arm—had escaped from the shawl in which it was wrapped, and was feebly embracing the mother's waist.

The sight of that small clinging hand brought a rush of tears to her eyes. There was compensation even here; there was something here between that sickly mother and child—there wasn't much to show for it, only a crooning voice and a wan smile and a little wasted clinging hand—that would last longer than the Stoics, that would last 'to and through the Doomsday fire.'

Strangely softened by this every-day sight, Lucy crept up the wide stone staircase to find Nurse Brannan. She looked so lost that a man going up, a medical student, asked her where she was going, and took her to the ward where Miss Brannan was nurse.

'I am afraid the doctors are going their rounds,' he said, as he looked in at the door, 'but I will take you into Miss Brannan's room, and you can wait there.'

He led Lucy through the ward—a large, delightful chamber, well lighted and cheerful, and with quite a bank of tall palms and ferns on a table near the door, an oasis of verdure for tired eyes to feast upon.

Lucy saw all this at a glance, and she saw also a group of men round a bed, and the nurses standing near, and she crept softly into Nurse Brannan's room.

She had time before the nurse came to her to see what a nurse's room was like. It was a tiny bit of a room partitioned off the ward, and it seemed all walls and ceiling. There was a little floor room, however, and a big window that went nearly up to the ceiling.

It was not unlike a room in a woman's college, only that there were texts on the walls, and there are no texts on the walls of the Stoics.

The occupant of the room must have understood Latin and Greek, for there were texts in both these languages. There was one text only in our common tongue, and that was over the mantelpiece. It was not an illuminated text, and it had no lovely floral border. It was written in plain, bold characters in black and white: 'Inasmuch as ye do it unto the least of these My brethren, ye do it unto Me.'

Lucy couldn't keep her eyes off those familiar words which she read now in a new light. There wasn't much else in the room to look at. There was a bed that was a couch by day; it was a bed still, though it was past eleven o'clock; Nurse Brannan had evidently not long risen from it. The room was in the disorder of the early morning, and the day arrangements did not yet prevail. It was as untidy as a nurse's room well could be: the breakfast things were still on the table, and the demure little bonnet and cloak looked as if they had hastily been taken off and thrown on the bed, and a pair of outdoor shoes were lying in the middle of the floor.

While Lucy was still noticing these details Nurse Brannan came in.

She was a little bit of a nurse, with pink cheeks and steady blue eyes and fluffy hair. She was not at all a formidable person.

Lucy ran up to her when she came in, and took both her hands. She couldn't ask the question that was on her lips, she was moved out of all sense and reason. The anxieties of the night and the mathematics of the morning, and the lean little encircling arm had moved her strangely, and now she was hardly master of herself.

Nurse Brannan shook her head.

'He is no better,' she said.

She didn't say it at all sadly. She was so used to such things — to sickness and suffering and death — it didn't move her in the least.

'I have just come back from St. Benedict's, and there is no improvement. He has had a dreadful night. They thought at one time of calling up the Tutor.'

'And they have not told him yet?' Lucy asked, pale to the lips. 'Are they going to let him die?'

'They have not told him; they have not told anyone in the college; but I don't know about letting him die.'

'You think he'll get over it? Oh, do you really think it possible with that — that dreadful wound he can get better?'

Only talking about the wound made Lucy sick and faint. She was made of very poor stuff. She would have been no good at Addenbroke's.

Nurse Brannan smiled.

'The wound is nothing,' she said: 'it is not at all serious. He will get better if he is well watched, and they protect him from himself. When the attack passes off he will not be much the worse — only it may occur again at any time.'

'The attack?' Lucy said feebly; she was quite at sea as to Nurse Brannan's meaning.

'Oh, you didn't know he did it in a fit of delirium tremens. This is the second time he has had an attack, and he has attempted his life both times. His friends ought to take him away and put him under restraint.'

Lucy didn't know what delirium tremens meant; happily she had been spared all her life from such miserable knowledge. She vaguely knew it was a 'possession' of some kind, an awful 'possession' like that which used to seize the men of old.

'You think the fit will pass?' she said.

'Oh yes; there is no reason why it shouldn't pass, and then the less they say to him about it the better. It would be well if he never knew; but the scar will remain, they cannot cover up that. There is no reason why he shouldn't be well enough to take his Tripos and go "down." The best thing that can happen to him will be to "go down."'

'Go down'—he looked very much more like going 'up,' Lucy thought, as she recalled the white face on the pillow; but she was immensely relieved by the nurse's assurance.

'And you have seen him this morning?' she said.

'Yes; I ran over for a minute directly I got up. I was not up till late. A woman was dying in the ward, and I stayed with her till she died. She did not die till daylight, and then I lay down for a few hours; and I had just time to snatch some breakfast and run over to St. Benedict's before the doctors came their rounds. I was only just back in time. I had to throw my things down and put on my slippers—I hadn't even time to put my cap straight. They were waiting for me in the ward when I came back. Oh dear! what a mess I left my room in!'

Her pretty plaited nurse's cap, that ought to be worn in the most demure fashion, that ought to be as straight as those lines of that detestable blackboard, was all awry, was positively jaunty, and her fluffy hair was quite outrageous. She didn't look the least like a real, staid nurse who is called upon to face death at any moment, and is always doing dreadful disagreeable things. She might have been playing at nursing, only her eyes were steady, and her lips had a great calm about them; they didn't quiver, and tremble, and curl, and ripple with laughter, like other girls.

Lucy was almost angry with her for the cool, not to say unfeeling, way in which she spoke of these dread realities—death and suffering. 'She has no heart!' she said to herself as she went back over the Fens to Newnham.

'Nurses are so used to pain that they have no sympathy. I wouldn't be a nurse for the world!' Then she remembered the words over the mantelpiece: 'Inasmuch——.' Was this the secret of that little fluffy, girlish nurse's hardness and endurance?

They don't do very much for other people at Newnham; and they do nothing for each other. They positively ignore each other. Perhaps this is owing to culture—the higher culture—and it hadn't reached Addenbroke's yet.

Lucy had written to the Tutor of St. Benedict's when she got back the previous day, excusing herself, in an incoherent fashion, for not keeping her appointment, and promising to come to his rooms at the same hour the next day.

She knew her way quite well this time, and she was five minutes before the hour she had appointed. The Senior Tutor's door was closed, and the way was quite clear. There was not a soul on the staircase; there was not a soul in the passage. Lucy could not resist the desire to knock at that closed door at the end of the passage, and find out for herself how the man was. She hadn't much faith in that thick-skinned little nurse; she would see for herself.

She knocked at the door at the end of the passage in her futile way, but of course nobody answered. If she had wasted all her strength upon it, it would have been the same thing, as the inmates of that mysterious room only gave admittance to privileged individuals upon preconcerted signals.

Lucy hadn't got the secret of that 'Open sesame,' and she was turning away. She hadn't got to the end of the passage, when the door really did open and someone came out. It was the bed-maker with a tray. Somebody had been having a meal, and she was carrying the débris away. Lucy stopped her at the end of the passage, and the two women stood looking at each other—the bed-maker suspiciously, and Lucy eagerly. There was no mistaking the anxious eagerness in Lucy's eyes.

'How is he?' she asked, more with her eyes than her lips, and she laid her detaining hand on the woman's arm. There must have been some Freemasonry in the touch, for the bed-maker softened, and the look of suspicion gave place to one of pity.

'He's quieter,' she said in a whisper, drawing Lucy back into the passage, out of sight of the Tutor's door; 'but he's been orful bad all the morning. As much as two of 'em could do to keep him in bed. It's a sad pity, miss, and such a nice gentleman—there isn't his fellow in the college!'

The bed-maker sniffed; she would have wept, no doubt, but she held a tray, and it would have been inconvenient, so she sniffed instead, and regarded Lucy with a watery eye. She evidently thought Lucy was his sweetheart.

Lucy took a coin from her slender purse and laid it on the tray. She didn't give it to anybody in particular, she only laid it on the tray, and the bed-maker curtsied.

'Will you ask Mr. Gwatkin if I may come in?' she said — 'the lady who was with him yesterday.'

She didn't give her name, but the woman knew her quite well — every bed-maker in St. Benedict's knew her. She wasn't the least surprised at the Master's niece taking an interest in one of her gentlemen — the nicest gentleman in the college. She had a tender spot in her withered bosom, under that rusty old shawl, and she was quite flustered at an *affaire de cœur* on her staircase.

She toddled back, tray and all, and by a preconcerted signal the door was opened, and she said a few words to someone inside, and then Eric Gwatkin came out into the passage and led Lucy in and closed the doors behind her.

He was looking dreadfully tired, she thought, and there were quite deep lines on his face; he seemed to have aged since yesterday. Perhaps it was with want of sleep, but Lucy put it down at once to his guilty conscience. She was feeling old herself, years older than yesterday.

'He has had a very bad night,' Eric Gwatkin said, speaking in a low voice and with his lips twitching, 'such a night as I pray God I may never witness again. You were not praying for us last night. You did not pray for him — for me — when you went away.'

Lucy bowed her head; she remembered she had not prayed for these men. What were they to her that she should pray for them?

She had been walking about the passages and frightening Pamela out of her wits instead, when she ought to have been on her knees.

The screen had been moved since yesterday; it had been drawn nearer the bed, so that the middle of the room where they were standing was left clear.

'He does not like to see anyone whispering,' Eric explained; 'he is very suspicious, and the least thing excites him.'

'You were alone with him all night?' Lucy asked, with a perceptible quiver in her voice; 'you have been up two nights.'

'That doesn't matter,' he said, 'I shall have all the strength I need; but last night he was very violent, and—and I thought I should have to call Mr. Colville. It was a great temptation—I could hardly resist it.'

'Oh, why didn't you?' said Lucy. 'Why do you take all this responsibility upon yourself?'

Eric Gwatkin smiled. His smile was not the least like Pamela's. Lucy couldn't help thinking, as she stood there, how it would change Pamela's face and take the weariness out of it if she had that smile.

'I don't mind the responsibility,' he said, 'or the anxiety, if I can save him. It would be worse than death to him to have it known. Oh, I think you must go home and pray that he may be brought through this, and may be kept for the future. He will need all our prayers.'

'What on earth are you whispering about, Wattles? I wish you would speak so that a fellow can hear what you are saying.'

The voice came from behind the screen—an impatient voice, not weak by any means.

'All right, old man; Miss Rae has come to ask how you are. He saw you yesterday,' he said, turning to Lucy and speaking in a lower voice; 'he remembered you quite well.'

'It's awfully good of you,' Wyatt Edgell said as Lucy came from behind the screen; 'I'm afraid we don't look like receiving visitors. Old Wattles here insists upon making a mess.'

He was lying back on the pillow with a wet bandage round his head, and a basin of lotion and some rags on a chair beside the bed. His shirt was torn open as if in a struggle, and his chest was bare. There was a scarf round his throat, a large silk scarf striped with the colours of his college that concealed whatever was beneath. Lying there with his head thrown back and those wet bandages, and his chest open—his splendid manly chest with all the muscles exposed—he looked like a man stricken down with fever, or some head trouble; no one would have guessed what the scarf thrown so loosely around his neck concealed.

'I am so glad you are better,' said Lucy softly, coming over to the bed and bending over him; 'you ought to get well soon, you have got such a good nurse.'

'Old Wattles, yes; he's very well, only he persists in keeping me in such a mess.'

He took the bandages off his head as he spoke, and rolled them up into a ball, and flung them to the other end of the room, where they rolled under a heavy piece of furniture, and Wattles, or Gwatkin rather, had to go on his knees and fish them out.

'There!' he said, 'that will give Wattles an excuse for going on his knees. He has been going on his knees all night. He would be a good fellow if he weren't always preaching and praying.'

He rolled his head impatiently on one side, and flung the pillow after the bandages, and Lucy, looking down upon him, saw a dark light in his eyes she had never seen in any eyes before. It wasn't exactly terror, but it was disgust and loathing and impatience.

'I beg your pardon,' he said, 'but there was a creature on that—a toad. I hate toads!' He shuddered as he spoke, and his eyes followed the direction of the pillow. 'It's there now! I wish Wattles would put it outside. It's been here all night.'

Gwatkin took up the pillow and shook it, and appeared to take something off it, and opened the window and made a gesture as if he had thrown the thing into the court below.

'There, old man,' he said reassuringly, 'it's gone now. It can't trouble you any more.'

And then he brought back the pillow, and Lucy put it under the poor fellow's head while he supported it, and she arranged it and smoothed it as only a woman's hand can arrange a pillow.

When she had done this, she put on the wet bandages afresh and bathed his head, and as she bathed it the dark light seemed to fade out of his eyes.

'You are very good,' he said with a sigh; 'you have exorcised that hideous little beast. It is gone now'—and he looked round the room fearfully—'quite gone.'

'Thank God!' said Gwatkin. 'Your visit has done some good, Miss Rae, if it has dispelled that hideous nightmare that has been pursuing him all night. I think he will sleep now.'

'I'm sure you ought to sleep yourself,' Lucy said, as she suddenly remembered the time and began dragging on her gloves. 'It is quite gone,' she said to Edgell, bending down over the bed; 'I am going to pick it up as I go out and carry it away.'

Having told this little fib, she went out, and Gwatkin closed the two doors after her.

She had to tell another fib or two when she went into the Tutor's room. He had been waiting for her exactly fifteen minutes, and he had waited an hour the day before.

She was absent and distrait all through the lesson; she was thinking about the man in the next room, and the creature she had promised to pick up in the court.

The Senior Tutor had never coached such an unpromising pupil. She would never get through her Little-go, he told himself—never, never. She would get plucked to a certainty.

Oh, it would never do for the future Mistress of St. Benedict's to be plucked!

He debated with himself while he was bending over her, and remarking what a dainty little profile it was, and how the little rings of chestnut hair clustered on her forehead, and how clear, how deliciously transparent, was the carnation tint of her cheek, and the shapely curve of her throat—such a little throat he could clasp it with his hand—he debated with himself, as he remarked these quite every-day things that no man in his senses except an old bachelor Fellow of a college would have noticed, whether it would not be better to settle the thing at once, and stop all this unprofitable work.

If Lucy knew what was before her, she would have other opportunities of fitting herself for her high position besides poring over mathematics, for which she clearly had no vocation.

'I'm afraid you find the work rather hard,' he said with a preliminary 'H'm' and 'Ah' to clear his throat. He didn't know exactly how to begin. What comes by nature at thirty is uncommonly hard at sixty. It is like going in again for a hurdle-race, or taking the high jump. He could have done it easily years ago, but he couldn't do it now. He stopped with that preliminary 'Ah.'

'Yes,' said Lucy, 'it is not very easy, but I am going to work eight hours a day. It is more than a month to the exam.; if I work very hard eight hours every day, I think I may manage it.'

Eight hours a day for a whole month! She was so much in earnest; and when she lifted her little pale drooping face to his, with just a suspicion of a tear on her eyelashes, he was really sorry for her. He was very near taking her in his arms and kissing away that fugitive tear and settling the matter— he was never nearer in his life.

Perhaps it was the best thing he could have done, but he missed the chance, and Lucy picked up her books and began to talk about the work she was to prepare for the next lesson.

'I wouldn't work eight hours a day,' he said; 'you will get through easier than that. I would give an extra two hours to tennis.'

He had never given a man this advice—perhaps it was not needed. He watched her, out of his window, cross the court. She did not happen to pick up the thing by the way as she had promised. Her step was less elastic, he noticed, than it used to be, and her face was paler—paler and thinner. She would never, never be young again, and life would never open afresh. There is only one young life, one time of roses, one sweet blossoming time, and it was just a question in the Tutor's mind, as he watched Lucy cross the court, whether the loss of this were worth all the mathematics in the world.

# CHAPTER IX
# A WOMAN'S PARLIAMENT

Lucy saw Pamela Gwatkin once only during the day, and that was at dinner. She only caught a far-off glimpse of her at the High table. Pamela very often sat at the 'High' among the Dons. The younger Dons were very fond of her: her opinions kept pace with theirs—they were very advanced opinions—and sometimes they outran them. She would be a Don herself some day, and she would be a pioneer in quite a new school of thought.

Lucy watched her with a feeling of awe as she sat among those great minds eating gooseberry pie—Lucy wouldn't have sat there for the world. The presence of so much learning would have taken away her appetite. The presence of the Master of St. Benedict's at the dinner-table never took away her appetite, but the dear old thing never talked above her head. He was very fond of recalling those old days, as he sat at meat, when Dick—not Lucy's father, but her great-grandfather—used to drive a team afield, and his good wife kept the stall in the butter market.

But the President and the Dons of 'Newe' never discussed such commonplace topics. They talked of literature, philosophy, science, with a fine breadth of handling which is peculiar to a woman's college. Pamela Gwatkin was in her right place among them.

There was the weekly political meeting held after Hall—a little miniature House of Commons—where the affairs of the nation were discussed, a foretaste of what will be by-and-by, when things are rearranged.

When the House took its seat at nine o'clock, Lucy found herself in the Opposition, and a long way off from the benches occupied by the Government of the country.

Lucy only represented an insignificant little borough that nobody else would stoop to represent. She had a little freehold in it—her only freehold— six feet of earth beneath the east window of her father's church at Thorpe Regis. Most people have a freehold of this sort, but it does not always give them a voice in the affairs of the nation. Lucy was returned unopposed on the strength of her little freehold, and as her views, if she had any, were not at all advanced, she found herself in the minority.

Pamela Gwatkin, or, as the girls called her, Newnham Assurance, was the Leader of the House, and Annabel Crewe Secretary for the Colonies, and Capability Stubbs had been unanimously elected Chancellor of the Exchequer; every girl that was worth anything had a place in the Cabinet.

Lucy hadn't much interest in the business that was going on, and she took out her knitting and turned the heel of a sock while the great affairs of the State were being discussed.

It was quite clear from what she did gather from the speeches on the Ministerial side that the country had been misgoverned long enough by the feeble race of men. It was quite time there was a change. A great deal of time had been lost; ages had been lost in the history of the world. Men had been first in the field; women took a longer time to ripen. They had ripened now; they were quite, quite ripe; they were ready for the change.

Oh, it was beautiful to hear the girls speak! There is an idea among narrow-minded people that debating societies encourage volubility of speech. Perhaps they do among men, and the practice of public speaking is apt to make them too loquacious, too apt to air their elementary knowledge and crude information in senseless verbiage. But garrulity is not the sin of the students of colleges for women. They not only know a great deal more than men know, but they have the delightful gift of ready and accurate language. They do not haggle and hesitate, and 'H'm' and 'Ah,' and have that dreadful difficulty in finding words that even prevails in a real House of Commons.

It was remarkable to see with what ease the Newnham girls handled those topics which old-fashioned legislators have been puzzling over Session after Session. There was a certain fine breadth in their way of handling them that would have taken a Conservative Leader's (the Leader of a real House of Commons) breath away.

It didn't take anybody's breath away in the Ladies' Parliament. Everybody knitted and listened unmoved, and when eleven o'clock came two very important Bills that had been brought forward from last Session were advanced a stage.

There was an exciting division before the House separated, that resulted in an overwhelming majority for the motion, 'That the Legal Profession and the Church be thrown open to women.'

That foolish little Lucy voted in the minority; there were not a dozen girls in Newnham who showed such a poor spirit, and of these five, it was rumoured, were engaged to curates.

The girls ran off to their rooms when the sitting of the House was ended in the highest possible spirits. Some of them sang snatches of songs, and some caught each other round the waist and waltzed madly down corridors. The thing was practically settled. The Bar and the Church opened vistas, immense vistas, for every sort of talent, and especially for the kind of talent that Newnham produced.

There would have to be more colleges for women—Newnham and Girton could not turn out nearly enough—there would have to be a great many Newnhams. Some girls, no doubt, sat down at once and began to prepare a sermon, and others took down Blackstone and began seriously to study law.

Lucy went back to her room alone. The Chancellor of the Exchequer, though she 'kept' next door, wouldn't take the slightest notice of her. She had lighted her lamp, and was just thinking what she would give for a cup of tea, when someone knocked at her door. It wasn't a girl with a cup of tea, as she hoped it might be—the Chancellor of the Exchequer, with all her fine airs, generally brought her in a cup of tea before she went to bed, and sometimes she condescended to sit down for five minutes and discuss the burning questions of the day. It was not the Chancellor of the Exchequer—it was a far greater person—it was the Leader of the House.

'Well?' she said, when she came in and had shut the door after her— 'well?'

She had come in so suddenly, and Lucy's mind was so full of the motion of the evening—this Parliamentary business was quite a new thing to her, and she had taken it *au serieux*—that she could not collect herself sufficiently to think what Pamela meant. Her mind was so full of the lady curates and the female barristers that she looked up at the Leader of the House in bewilderment.

'Well,' said Pamela impatiently, 'how is he? I saw by your face at Hall that he was not dead. Is he going to get well?'

Then Lucy remembered all about it.

'Oh dear!' she said, 'how could I have forgotten! Yes, he is going to get well, I think. He will owe his life if he does to Eric. Oh, Eric has been lovely!'

'Eric has done no more than anyone else would have done,' Pamela said coldly; 'no more than a woman would have done if a woman had been in his place.'

'I don't think a woman *could* have done what Eric has done,' Lucy said.

She was thinking of those stitches he had put in, and how he had struggled with the poor fellow all night, and how he had been watching and praying beside him for two whole nights and days.

Nurse Brannan would have done as much as most women, but she would not have done all this.

'Oh, you don't know what women can do!' Pamela said, with a little curl of her lip. Her lips were so thin and so hard—such crisp lips that they couldn't help curling. 'You are only a fresher; when you have been here three years you will have found out what a woman can do. He would never have cut his throat if a woman had been near him.'

'No,' said Lucy eagerly, 'I am sure he wouldn't—not if a woman he loved had been near. Oh dear! you should have seen the wistfulness in his poor eyes when I put the wet bandage on his head! It was enough to melt one's heart. Eric says he will be sure to do it again—at least, that we must never leave off praying for him. I am sure that there is only one thing that can save him from doing it again.'

'Only one thing?' Pamela repeated, with just an inflection of scorn in her voice. 'And what is this panacea for his wickedness and folly? What is this fine thing that is to save him from himself?'

'Don't speak of it so lightly; it is not a little thing!'

There were tears in Lucy's voice as she spoke, and in her eyes. She had the picture before her of the strong man, with his beautiful bare chest, and his splendid frame, and those wistful eyes, and the loathing and the dread with which he shrank from the creature on his pillow. The pity of it was strong upon her, and she was deeply moved.

'A great love would save him—the love of a good woman. He would do a great thing for a woman he loved; he would make any sacrifice. I don't think anything else would save him.'

The Leader of the House of Commons turned from white to pink. Lucy might have been talking about her. She wore a very pretty white gown of some soft silky stuff, and it was folded across the bosom, and the folds heaved up and down as Lucy spoke, as if she were breathing heavily.

'Perhaps he has done this for a woman's sake,' she said bitterly. 'Men are such fools! they will do anything for a woman's sake—not always a worthy woman.'

'I am sure he has not!' said Lucy hotly. 'He has been working too hard, and he has broken down. I heard at the lodge that he was working ten hours a day; that he was certain to come out first. Oh, you don't know how they are building upon him at St. Benedict's! It isn't a woman—it's overwork.'

Pamela smiled.

'You are a capital champion, my dear, only don't suffer yourself to get too much interested in this foolish young man; it will interfere with your work. You must not make a mistake and let pity drift into—love.'

She made a little pause before the word, and the colour came again into her cheeks. She looked ever so much prettier talking about pity—and love—than she did speaking on those troublesome Bills that had already occupied the time of two Sessions.

'Oh, he is never likely to love me!' said Lucy. 'He could only love his equal; no one else would have any influence over him. He would only love a queen among women.'

'Perhaps he has found his queen already. Most men have before they are twenty-three.'

The colour went out of the girl's face, and the cold light came back into her eyes, and her lips, that a moment before were tremulous and tender, were hard and firm.

'I wouldn't go too often to Mr. Edgell's rooms, if I were you, dear,' she said when she went away. 'The authorities would make a fuss if they heard of it. We are not supposed, you know, to visit a man's room without a chaperon. I don't think it would do to take a chaperon there. If you have any more interest in him, I will find out for you how he is going on from Eric.'

'Thank you,' said Lucy warmly; 'I can find out for myself. I can hear all about the St. Benedict's men at the lodge.'

She was quite frightened at herself for speaking in that way to the Prime Minister. She had got into the way now, since she had been at Newnham, of taking her own part; she was beginning to have no respect for dignities.

# CHAPTER X
# 'THAT CONFOUNDED CUCUMBER!'

Lucy didn't go to Wyatt Edgell's room again. She caught sight of the friendly bed-maker once or twice on the staircase when she went to Mr. Colville's room to be coached in mathematics, and she held a little whispered conference with her on the stairs.

Edgell was better: he was up again and at work—working very hard, the woman said (and bed-makers know something about work). He was 'going on as quiet and as steady as any gentleman on the staircase.' This verdict from such a quarter was as good as a college testimonial.

When there is a mixed University, and a lady President at the lodge, and a female Vice-Chancellor, and the affairs of the Senate are conducted by dowagers, bed-makers will no doubt be required to sign college testimonials.

The first time Lucy saw Wyatt Edgell after that day when she put the wet bandage round his head, and promised to pick up the dreadful thing Eric had thrown out of window, and carry it away with her, was at the college chapel.

It was a fortnight after the day when she had picked him out from among all the men of St. Benedict's as Pamela Gwatkin's brother. He was sitting in the same place, and he was very little changed; he was paler, Lucy thought, and he was muffled up round the throat for that warm May day. She couldn't help looking at him. Her eyes would wander over to the bench where he sat, do what she would to keep them fixed in quite an opposite direction.

The Master took such a long time over the Litany that morning. He had read it for so many years in that college chapel, Sunday after Sunday, but he had never read it so slowly as he was reading it to-day. The men yawned and fidgeted as he read, and the old fellows in the stalls opposite looked across with grave, questioning eyes—they would have to elect another Master shortly—and the women-folk kneeling by his side looked up anxiously; but Lucy's eyes had wandered again to the end seat on the last bench, while her lips were murmuring:

'"That it may please Thee to raise up them that fall, and finally to beat down Satan under our feet."'

Wyatt Edgell looked up while she was praying for him—she was distinctly praying for him, she had prayed this very prayer for him every night and morning since Eric had told her how he needed her prayers—and their eyes met.

Lucy was covered with confusion. She was quite sure in that swift momentary glance that he had read her inmost thoughts. She was ashamed that he should know that she had been praying all this time that he should be strengthened and comforted and helped and picked up again when he fell, and that the enemy should be beaten down under his feet. She never looked at that end of the chapel again all the rest of the service.

It was over at last—the long, long Litany and the slow, faltering prayers: the men need not have been so restless, they would not hear them much longer. The old walls would echo another voice soon, and the feeble lips would be repeating another Litany elsewhere.

The old college chapel was full of echoes and shadows; there would be another shadow shortly, and the echo of a tremulous, quavering voice would join those other ancient echoes in the roof. It was a dark, gloomy old chapel; it had been built for hundreds of years, and it was full of old memories. Every bench and stall and desk had a memory of its own, stretching back, far back, into quite early ages—memories of old Masters and Fellows and scholars and undergraduates who had worshipped there through, oh! so many generations.

There was a musty smell of old Masters rising up from the vaults beneath and pervading the chapel, and in the ante-chapel beyond there were monuments on the walls, and brasses—quite lovely old brasses—on the pavement, and great hideous tombs of long dead and gone Masters and Fellows. It was touching to see how they were forgotten after a generation or two; how even their very tomb-stones were hidden away in a corner, and covered up with organ pipes. There was the marble effigy of an old, old Master, whose learning and virtues were recited in a long Latin epitaph on an elaborate tablet hidden away behind the organ.

Everyone had forgotten him years ago, and his old monument was in the way, and so they had covered it up. Music is so much more delightful than old memories. They will all be swept away soon, and a new chapel will be built. There will be no old memories and old ghosts and old storied windows, no decaying woodwork or musty odour of old Masters. It will all be fresh and bright and sweet-smelling and shiny as new paint and varnish can make it, and there will be a new organ with electric stops. It will be dark and shadowy no longer; the old echoes and the old ghosts will all be scared away—they will vanish quite away in the blaze of the new electric lamps with which the chapel will be lighted.

Lucy vanished out of the college chapel almost as rapidly as the ghosts will by-and-by. She did not linger in the cloisters to-day. She hurried back to the lodge, and left Cousin Mary and the Master's wife to toddle back beside the Master.

'How do you think your uncle looks to-day, my dear?' the old lady asked Lucy when they had got him safely back to the lodge, and had put him in his great armchair, and given him some wine.

There was a shade of anxiety in her voice as she asked the question. Lucy hadn't seen the Master for a week, so she might have been expected to notice any change in him.

'Oh, I think he looks lovely, aunt! He walked back from chapel quite strong.'

Mrs. Rae shook her head; she was not quite convinced.

'There were two of us supporting him, my dear, one on either side, and I thought he leant rather heavily.'

He had nearly crushed the poor little soul into the ground; she could not have supported his weight a dozen steps more.

'Perhaps you are not so strong yourself to-day, auntie dear; you are looking pale. Most likely the weakness is yours, and you are not so well able to bear his weight. He always leans heavily; I often wonder how you and Mary can keep him up!'

'Perhaps so, my dear. I hope it may be so!' But still the cloud on the dear old face did not quite vanish. 'I fancied that his reading in chapel was slower to-day than usual—that his voice was weak. Did you notice it?'

'Oh yes; I noticed that he read lovely! I never heard him read so well as he read to-day.'

'You really think so? I am very glad! The fault must be in me. I don't think I am quite so strong to-day—I can't expect to be at my age; but I am very glad there is nothing unusual the matter with the Master. You would have been quite sure to have noticed it, my dear, if there had been, as you haven't seen him for a week.'

She kissed that mendacious little Lucy and tottered out of the room. She was very feeble to-day—perhaps the Master's weight had been too much for her; but there was quite a glad smile on her patient face. She was so happy, the brave old soul, to feel that the weakness was hers, not his.

Wyatt Edgell went back straight from chapel to his own rooms. He met Eric coming out of chapel, and they went back together.

'Where have I seen that girl before?' he asked Eric when they got back to the room.

'Oh, you've often seen her in chapel. She's the Master's niece, or grand-niece, or something of the kind,' said Eric evasively.

But the other was not so easily put off.

'I have seen her somewhere else, besides in chapel,' he said thoughtfully. 'I've seen her in this room. I've seen her beside my bed. Good heavens! Wattles, you didn't let that girl in—when—when——'

'When you weren't quite yourself, old man,' said Eric cheerfully, filling up the gap. 'What on earth should the Master's niece come in here for? Be reasonable, and don't ask such foolish things!'

'Foolish or not, I'll be hanged if I didn't see her in this room, standing where you stand now! You may as well tell the truth, Wattles. You may as well say you called her in and showed her the spectacle!'

He was a very determined-looking young man, and he didn't look like one to be trifled with, as he stood with his back to the empty fireplace, leaning against the mantelpiece, and his great hands stuck down well in his pockets.

'Dear old man, you may take my word for it: I did not call her in; I should as soon have thought of calling the Master in!'

'I wish to Heaven you had called the Master in—I should have known the worst then; but for this girl to see me—in—in that state!'

He paused and groaned, and two upright lines came out on his forehead.

'You take too much for granted, old man,' said the other; but he couldn't put any heartiness into his voice. 'Haven't I told you that not a soul in the college but Brannan and myself came into the room—while—while you were ill?'

'Yes,' said the other moodily—'not a soul in the college; but this girl from Newnham came in. I'll swear it! I saw it in her eyes.'

It was no use Eric pretending. Edgell was not in a mood to be trifled with. He was a great big, determined fellow. He could have taken Eric up and flung him to the other end of the room with the same ease with which he had flung the pillow.

'Go on,' he said moodily; 'go on, and tell me all about it. Tell me why this girl came in, and the spectacle she saw. Let me know exactly the degradation to which I have sunk!'

There was no help for it. Eric had to tell him all about Lucy's visit—Lucy's second visit; he didn't say anything about the first. How could he tell the poor fellow that she had come in at that dreadful time; that it was her hands that had wiped up all the traces of his crime; that it was she who had helped him when he had put those stitches in that gaping wound in his throat!

Eric told him quite enough. His head had fallen forward on his breast, and he looked a picture of despondency. A despondent giant of six feet, with a great broad chest, and big muscular limbs, and a splendid head splendidly set on a splendid full white throat—it was muffled up now, but it was as white and shapely as a woman's beneath the crisp, close-cut whisker curling down below the cheek. His chin and his great square jaw were close-shaven, but there was a thin, slight, crisp moustache on his upper lip, and his short hair curled crisply at the edges. He wore it parted in the middle, not very neatly parted, and tossed back off his forehead. Everything about him denoted strength and courage—such a man could not be despondent long.

'Then she knows the worst,' he said—'the very worst. There is nothing else she has got to learn about me. There is only one thing to be done, Wattles, with a girl who knows so much about me: I must marry her. You must introduce me again, old man, and I shall make her an offer, and—and she will marry me.'

His gloom and depression had quite gone, and he was smiling again. He was a delightful fellow when he smiled. Not a man in the college could resist that delightful smile; it disarmed the wrath of all the Dons, and it won the hearts of bed-makers.

'Marry her!' said Eric, turning quite pale. 'Dear old man, don't be in such a hurry. Think it over. She isn't the sort of woman for you, Edgell.'

Wyatt Edgell laughed. His laugh was a full-blown edition of his smile; but Gwatkin looked serious.

'Perhaps you'll tell me, Wattles, what is the sort of woman for me.'

'Oh, I wouldn't pretend to say; only, old man, don't trifle with this poor little thing. She's the sort of girl to break her heart for a man. I wouldn't break her heart if I were you.'

'Perhaps she'll break mine,' said Edgell dryly; and then he sat down and ate his lunch which the bed-maker had already spread out on the table.

It was a very nice college lunch. It was not tinned beef, or brawn, or tongue, or any questionable dainty that had been soldered up a year or two in a metal case. It was a lovely head and shoulders of salmon, and it had been judiciously pickled, and there was cucumber cut up in a dish—little delicate flakes of cucumber which Edgell ate with the healthy returning appetite of a man who had long been denied this delicacy.

The salmon was followed by a chicken and a ham, to which he also applied himself with the same zest. The edge was quite taken off his appetite, when Eric pushed these things aside and set a jelly just freshly turned out of a mould before him.

'I don't want any of that stuff,' he said, and he pushed over his glass in the direction of the claret.

'I don't think I'd take any more, old man,' said Eric; 'you've already had four glasses. I wouldn't have any more. Have a soda?'

'I'll be hanged if I do!' said the other doggedly, 'unless you put some brandy in it. I must have a nip of brandy, Wattles. I'm sure that cucumber has disagreed with me. I haven't had any cucumber for an age, and it never did agree with me.'

Eric got up and unlocked a cupboard, and took out a liqueur-bottle more than half full of brandy, and poured a small—a very small—quantity into a glass, and filled it up with seltzer-water.

He had put the bottle back into the cupboard and the key into his pocket, and was putting on his gown to go out. He always took a service somewhere in the country, or did some open-air preaching on Sunday afternoons, and he was in a hurry to get away.

'I wish you'd leave that key behind you, Wattles,' Edgell called out when he got to the door. 'That confounded cucumber or the pickled salmon has disagreed with me. I may want the key before you come back.'

Eric took the key out of his pocket reluctantly and laid it on the mantelpiece.

'You'll be careful, old man,' he said; 'you'll be sure to be careful. Remember——'

'Shut up!' said the other angrily. 'Do you think I'm such a fool?'

Eric went out and shut the door. When he came back two hours later the liqueur-bottle was on the table empty, and Edgell was breathing heavily on the floor.

It was all that confounded pickled salmon and cucumber!

# CHAPTER XI
# IN THE FELLOWS' GARDEN

That mendacious little Lucy, in spite of all her assurances to the Master's wife, was a little anxious about the Master. He had not taken his dinner with his usual appetite; he had scarcely eaten a morsel, and he had not had his usual nap after.

He had left half the wine in his glass, and he had got up from the table earlier than usual; but he had not fallen asleep in his chair after, as was his wont. He had sat talking to Lucy all the afternoon about the old time. His memory was wonderfully clear about the things that had happened, oh! so long ago—more than half a century before she was born—and he talked to her about them as if they had happened yesterday.

He was always so glad to see Cousin Dick's little daughter; she brought back the past to him, and seemed a link between the old far-off time and the present. He recalled to-day his very earliest years, his first remembrances. He recalled the time when his brother Dick carried him on his shoulders to the fair.

'It was Midsummer Fair, my dear,' he explained, 'and your father left off work early; he was very fond of fairs, and junketings, and wrestling matches. He liked bull-baiting, too. I mind the bull-ring at the end of the village on a piece of waste ground; I dare say it is there now. I've seen many a bull baited there in my day. There was never a fair within ten miles but your father was there in his best, with a flower in his button-hole—he always wore a flower in the button-hole of his plum-coloured coat. I remember that coat well; it had gilt buttons, and he wore a waistcoat to match, with two rows of buttons on either side—it was the fashion then, my dear. He carried me on his shoulder all the way to the fair; it was held on the green; there was a large green in the middle of the village in those days, but it is built over now; things have altered since then.'

The old Master shook his head and sighed. He hated changes of any kind; he would have liked the world to go on in the same old grooves for ever. He was silent for some time, and his watchful women-folk thought he was going to sleep—that he would have his after-dinner nap, after all; but he was only thinking. Those old chambers of memory were unlocked, and the old faces of his youth were crowding around him.

'Yes,' he said presently, brightening up, 'your mother was there, too, my dear. Dick met her in a dancing-booth. She wouldn't look at Dick at first, she had so many sweethearts. She was a proud little thing, with a spirit of her own; she nearly broke Dick's heart before he married her, but she made him a good wife—a good wife and a good mother, and always in her place in church, and bringing her children up to work and to fear God. I don't know that women do more in these days when they learn so many things.'

Lucy couldn't help thinking of that motion in the House of Commons, which was carried with such an overwhelming majority, that was to admit women to practise at the Bar and in the Church, to say nothing of those other learned professions that were already practically open.

The old Master's views were very, very old-fashioned; the world had made rapid strides while he had been sitting in his armchair and reading his Sunday Litanies in that musty old college chapel.

'Your father had a spirit of his own, too, my dear,' the old man babbled on with quite surprising vigour—these old memories made him quite young again; 'he wouldn't stay there to be slighted, with all the neighbours looking on. He left your mother going round with a young spark who had come down from London, and with me on his shoulder he went through the fair. I mind the booths quite well, with the gilt gingerbread, and the toys, and the trumpets, and the drums, and the merry-go-rounds. There was a show with a fat woman—I have never forgotten that fat woman. I have never seen anything like her since. There was a dwarf there, too—the smallest dwarf that was ever seen. I remember him strutting about the stage with his little sword; he wore a sword, and a gold-laced coat, and a cocked hat. The fat lady took his arm when the performance was over—she had to stoop down to do it, and he had to stretch up. I shall never forget seeing them go off the stage, arm-in-arm—the funniest sight I have ever seen—or how the people in the show laughed and clapped their hands when the showman made a ridiculous speech as they went out. "That's the way they go to church every Sunday of their lives!" he said, pointing after them. I believed him, if the crowd didn't, and for years after I used to watch the church door to see them coming in; but I have never seen them since.'

Lucy was so anxious about the old Master that when she went for her lesson to the Tutor's rooms the next day she could do nothing but talk about him.

The Tutor was anxious too, perhaps, in another way. He had noticed a change in the Master, and he went over to the lodge with her as soon as the lesson was over.

The Master was very feeble to-day, but he was up, and downstairs, and he was talking about going out into the garden. He was very fond of the old Fellows' Garden, and the seat beneath the walnut-tree—a sunny seat in the winter, a shady seat in the summer. It was shady now, but the garden was full of sunshine; the lilacs were in bloom, and the laburnums were a blaze of gold, and the thorn-tree was white with may. It was the blossoming time of the year, and everything was at its prime.

The Tutor took him out on his arm and sat him down on his old seat. He noticed how heavily he leant upon him as he tottered feebly across the grass. He would have crushed a woman with his weight. The Master's wife came out too, and sat by his side, with his hand in hers, and Lucy walked with the Tutor in the shady, winding paths beneath the trees. The trees were all old and gnarled, and some had broken down with age, and were propped up. The borders were full of old-fashioned flowers—perennials that went down into the earth every winter, and came up again every spring. There was nothing new here.

The Senior Tutor, as he walked by Lucy's side, was thinking how he should change all this by-and-by. He would cut down those useless old trees, and he would have the turf rolled and laid out for tennis. Nothing could be better for Lucy than tennis, and she could invite her Newnham friends. Those old flower borders should be all dug up, and some standard rose-trees planted. He would have nothing but first-rate sorts, the very latest. He would do away with that vulgar cabbage rose in the corner, and that poor, shabby little pale blush that hung in clusters on the wall. It had hung there for so many years; it was quite time it should be cleared away. It seemed a pity to lose time. There were so many improvements to be made; it seemed a pity not to begin now.

Looking across the grass and the sunshine at the old stooping figure under the walnut-tree—it was bent more than usual to-day—he could not but feel that the time was not far off when it would be there no longer. There was nothing pathetic in the sight to him. He had waited for the place—the Master's place—so long. If he waited much longer he would be feeble and old and white-haired, too.

There is little pathos in the young. The sad realities of life touch only those who know something about them. One must have suffered one's self to have any sympathy with suffering.

Lucy, looking across the sunshine, was touched, in spite of herself, at the group under the walnut-tree. It didn't affect her as it affected the Tutor. It would be no gain to her if the old Master were to die; it would mean loss and change and being driven out again homeless into the wide world.

But it was not this consideration that moved her. She was touched by the tender picture of the two brave, patient old souls sitting hand-in-hand in that calm closing evening of their life.

Here was a love that Lucy knew nothing about—a love that had weathered all the storms of life, and was burning brightly at its close. Riches and honour and learning were nothing to it. They were the Master's still, but they were nothing beside love. He would leave these behind him, but love would cling to him out of time. He wouldn't shake that off when he shook off everything else.

Lucy didn't put the idea into words, but it touched her; and then, strangely enough, rose up before her the face of the man who had sat on the last seat in the chapel and had caught her looking at him. It was quite ridiculous to think of Wyatt Edgell at such a moment; there was nothing here to remind her of him.

There was an old disused greenhouse at the end of the Fellows' garden. Nothing had grown in it for years. A neglected vine was dropping down from the roof in one corner, and a great deal of the glass was broken, and the woodwork was decayed and rotting. The Tutor shook the door as he passed, and it opened, and he paused and looked in.

'I think we must have this place rebuilt,' he said, thinking aloud. 'You would like a greenhouse. We must get some ferns and palms and foliage plants. Do you like foliage plants?'

'Not much,' Lucy said. She could not think what he meant by appealing to her. 'I like flowers best. I don't care for leaves. I'm afraid my taste is very vulgar. I like geraniums, and mignonette, and camellias; I am very fond of camellias. We used to have some in our greenhouse at home.'

'You can keep as many as you like here,' he said. 'We will get all the varieties there are, and you can have geraniums in flower all the year round.'

He shut the door, and they walked down the path together, while Lucy wondered what he could mean. It would be scarcely worth while to do up the old greenhouse and fill it with flowers when it was not likely she would be there another spring to see it.

In the long path they met Cousin Mary coming towards them. She looked rather pale and worn in the sunshine, and she had on a most unbecoming garden-hat. It had been hanging up in the hall all the winter; it might have been hanging there for years, and it was battered out of all shape. There was not a bed-maker in the college that would have worn it.

The Tutor had never noticed before how gray her hair had grown, and that there were crow's-feet round her eyes, and that her cheeks were faded. She had not changed lately. She had looked like this for years, getting a little grayer every year, and adding a line or two beneath her eyes, but he had never noticed it before. He was very fond of her still; he had the highest opinion of Mary Rae, but he was very glad that Lucy had come in time—just in time—to save him from throwing himself away.

'Mr. Colville is going to have the old greenhouse done up, Mary,' Lucy shouted to her when she was quite a dozen paces away. 'He's going to have camellias and geraniums all the year round; but perhaps you don't like camellias.'

The Senior Tutor for once in his life blushed. It was not for Mary he was going to have those geraniums in perennial bloom.

'I don't think it's worth it,' said Mary bluntly—'at least, not for us. We shall soon be going away.' And she looked in the direction of the walnut-tree beneath which the old Master and his wife were still sitting.

'That should make no change,' the Tutor said awkwardly; 'the lodge would be still your home.'

He grew ridiculously red, and he did not dare to look Mary in the face.

'We need not talk about that yet,' she said with a smile; 'the dear Master is still with us. I came to ask you to help him in; he has sat there long enough. He is not so strong to-day; I can't manage him alone.'

'I should think not!' said the Tutor, and he hurried off across the grass and took the old Master back to the lodge.

Lucy did not go in; she slipped through the garden-door into the court, and hurried back to Newnham. She had promised to drink tea in a girl's room, and she was already half an hour late.

She went back by way of the Fens, and when she was near the bridge she saw some figures she thought she knew crossing it, and they stopped while she came up, and looked down into the water.

It was Pamela Gwatkin and her brother, and there was another man with him. She had never seen Pamela with her brother before, and she was struck as she came up to them with the points of difference between them.

Being twins, they ought to have been exactly alike. Eric was short, and Pamela was tall—tall and graceful and slender, as a girl ought to be, with a proud, self-reliant bearing that is peculiar to the students of a college for women. Eric was not only short, but he was stout, and not at all graceful, and he had no bearing to speak of. He was an awkward, well-meaning, commonplace fellow. There was nothing remarkable about him whatever, except that he was Pamela's twin brother. This in his case was a decided disadvantage—the ingredients hadn't been properly mixed. All the masculine characteristics had gone to Pamela, and the tender, endearing qualities to her brother. He saw Lucy come tearing along across the Fen, and he took off his hat as she came up to him.

'You have met Eric before,' said Pamela, by way of introduction.

She was looking very pink and white and cool as she stood there on the bridge looking down into the dark shady water, and Lucy had run herself into a fever, and was hot and flushed, and looking 'hideous,' as she told herself.

'Oh yes,' she panted—she was quite out of breath with running in the hot sun—'I have met Mr. Gwatkin before.'

She didn't see, until Pamela's brother introduced her, that the other man leaning over the bridge was Wyatt Edgell. She was so flustered with running, and so taken by surprise, that she blushed like a peony.

She felt she was blushing furiously, and that Pamela, cool and critical and self-possessed, was watching her. Oh, how she hated herself for not being cool and dignified and self-possessed like other people!

They walked back over the Fen and through the lane to Newnham in couples, Lucy and Wyatt Edgell in front, Pamela and her brother behind. Lucy would have given the world to have reversed the order, but the man took his place by her side, and he wouldn't go away until he left her at the gate of Newnham.

'You have met me before, Miss Rae, as well as Gwatkin,' he said, as he walked by Lucy's side. 'I believe he invited you in to see the spectacle.'

'He didn't invite me in at all,' Lucy said hotly; 'I came in. You were very ill when I saw you; I did not expect you would get well so soon.'

'No?' he said indifferently, 'I suppose not. It did not much matter either way.'

'It mattered a great deal!' she said sharply. She was very angry with him for speaking in that absurd way—absurd and ungrateful—considering what a trouble he had been to his friends. 'It mattered a great deal to Mr. Gwatkin. Oh, you don't know how anxious he was about you! He saved your life.'

'Yes,' he said in his slow, indifferent way, flicking with his cane at the nettles in the hedge; 'I believe he did. It was rather a pity he should have taken so much trouble, but I suppose he liked it. I believe he didn't get off his knees all one night. He's always glad of an excuse for getting on his knees.'

And then he laughed. It was such a delightful laugh that it ought to have been infectious, but Lucy looked grave.

'I suppose he was on his knees when you came in?' he said.

'Yes,' said Lucy shortly, but she didn't tell him that she had knelt down beside Eric and prayed that the life he valued so little might be spared. She was very angry with him; she could only trust herself to say 'Yes.'

'Oh, he is a good fellow is Wattles, but he has his little crazes.'

'He is a splendid fellow!' said Lucy warmly.

She was ashamed of her warmth the moment after she had said it, but they had reached the gate of Newnham by this time, and she was glad to say 'Good-bye' and run away. She left him standing at the gate waiting for the others to come up, while quite a dozen girls on the lawn were looking at him and admiring him, and making up all sorts of fine stories in their heads about him.

If they had only known what Lucy knew about him they would have made up a great deal more.

# CHAPTER XII
# AN UGLY FALL

There was a row royal when Pamela got back to Newnham. She told Lucy that her conduct was disgraceful, and that if it came to the ears of the Dons she would be 'hauled.'

There had been several girls 'hauled' lately for the same offence—walking with an undergraduate to the very gate of the college.

Lucy mildly suggested that she was not exactly alone, that Pamela and her brother were with her, and that she herself, when she came up to her on the bridge, was walking in the young man's society.

'You forget that Eric was with me,' Pamela replied sharply. 'It makes all the difference if you have a brother, or any male relative, with you; but to be walking alone, tearing along at the rate you were, and talking confidentially—anyone could see that you were talking confidentially—dozens of girls have been sent down for less than that!'

Lucy wasn't 'hauled,' and she wasn't 'sent down'; but Pamela behaved like a bear to her for the remainder of the term.

Lucy was so anxious about the Master that she went over to the lodge the next day directly after lunch. Cousin Mary was out; she had left him sitting in his chair taking his after-dinner nap as usual, and she had gone out. He woke up directly Lucy came in, and began to talk to her about her father and the old time. She was very glad that she had not brought Pamela in with her, or any of the Newnham girls, as she sometimes did. He would have told them that ridiculous story that was running in his mind, how his brother Dick had met her mother at a dancing-booth at the fair. He would have dwelt on all the homely details of their humble history. It would have been all over Newnham the next day that her father was a ploughman, and her mother kept a stall in the butter-market. Annabel Crewe, who had a fine taste for caricature, would have drawn delightful pictures of Lucy's progenitors—a lovely old man in a smock-frock with straw round his legs, and a milkmaid with her pail!

She couldn't divert the Master's attention from this ridiculous topic. He had forgotten all about the things that had happened in later years, and had gone back in memory to the old familiar scenes and faces of his youth. His eyes were brighter to-day, and he was more restless than usual; he wanted to go out into the garden and sit in his accustomed seat on the lawn. It was such a perfect May day that no wonder he wanted to get out of that dark, gloomy old room, with the stuffy moreen curtains over the windows, and the faded carpets, and the worm-eaten, old-fashioned furniture, and the musty old books, into the sweet summer sunshine, where everything was fresh and new.

There was nothing dark and gloomy and oppressive out there in that sweet leafy Fellows' garden. The lilacs were in their prime, pale puce and white and purple, every delightful indescribable hue, and the laburnum was dropping gold upon the grass. There was a cuckoo somewhere, calling, and the thrushes were singing, and the blackbird's note was still shrill and clear. It would soon be hoarse as a raven's, and the thrush would be silent, and the cuckoo would have altered his tune, and the lilac would have faded, and the gold of the gleaming, down-dropping laburnums would have turned to gray—and—and he might not be here to see it. If he wanted to enjoy the fleeting sunshine and the flying blossoms of the year, there was no time like the present.

The Master didn't exactly put it in this way, but he was impatient to be out in the garden, in his old seat, and he wouldn't wait a minute longer for anybody.

If Mary wasn't there he would go without her.

There are none so impatient as the old. The young have plenty of time to spare—they have their life before them; but the old have not a minute to lose. The Master went out as usual, leaning on the arm that had supported him so many years, that had never failed him yet. Mrs. Rae and Lucy took him out between them. He walked in his slow accustomed way, leaning rather heavily on these two frail props until he reached his seat beneath the walnut-tree, and here he ought to have sat down.

But he didn't sit down. He insisted on going farther; he insisted on going down the path to the greenhouse. Mary had been saying something about it, repeating what the Tutor had said yesterday about having it done up and turned to some account, and the Master would not be satisfied until he had seen it. He must be consulted about it; nothing should be done in the gardens without his consent. He had been worrying about it all night.

He had got half-way down the path, when Lucy fancied he was beginning to lean heavily, more heavily than she could bear, though she put out all her strength. There was not a seat near, but she stopped and begged the Master to rest awhile. He was so anxious to see the greenhouse that he would not listen to her. He never thought of the women who were being weighed down with his great weight. He was as eager and determined as a child.

'I am sure, aunt, you are not strong enough to keep him up,' Lucy said in despair; she was getting really frightened. 'We must get someone to help him back. Oh, if someone would only come in!'

There was not a gardener in sight, and it was not likely that anyone would come in. Nobody but the Fellows ever walked in that garden.

The Master tottered on, feebler at every step; but he would not be kept back, and the two frightened women held him up as well as they could. He seemed to want more support every step he took; he was as feeble and helpless as a child, but still he pressed on. Lucy was sure she couldn't bear the strain a minute longer, and the dear old mistress was straining with all her might to keep up with him. She was putting out all her strength. It wasn't much to put out at the best, but she didn't keep back a feather weight. Oh, if someone would only come!

They came in sight of that wretched greenhouse at last, and here the Master stopped. He didn't exactly stop, but he tottered forward, and Lucy with a supreme effort kept him up, and with all his weight upon her he swayed to and fro, and before she knew what was happening he had slipped through her arms to the ground. He lay on the path, as he fell, all of a heap. He had no power to help himself, and he lay panting and breathing heavily as he had fallen, and the women stood beside him wringing their hands.

Lucy didn't stand beside him long. There was a door in the wall beside the greenhouse that led out into one of the courts, and she flew over to it. Fortunately the door was unlocked. Lucy looked eagerly round the deserted court and raised her feeble cry for help. It was such a feeble, piteous cry; it was like a wail. A man sitting reading at an open window looked out at that strange sound, and Lucy called to him: 'Oh, come, come, do come!'

The man didn't stay to ask what had happened; he was at Lucy's side in another moment, and she took him in through the open door to where the Master lay. It was Wyatt Edgell. A gyp coming across the court had heard the cry for help, and between them they bore the Master back to the lodge.

When Mary Rae came in she found a little anxious group gathered round him, and Wyatt Edgell was trying to reassure the frightened women.

Nothing very serious had happened. No bones were broken, but the Master was very much shaken, and he was not quite himself. Wyatt Edgell stayed with him until the doctor had come, and had ascertained that things were not very bad—not so bad as they might have been—and had calmed the fears of the women; and then Lucy was so shaken that he walked back with her to Newnham.

Lucy certainly would have been 'hauled' if the Dons had seen her walking back leaning heavily on an undergraduate's arm. She would have been invited to an interview with the authorities in the Principal's room, and she would have received a caution, perhaps a reprimand, and she would have been very lucky if nothing worse had happened. Lucy forgot all about the Dons and Pamela's warning. She only thought about that poor old man at the lodge.

'I don't think he will ever get over this,' she said, or rather sobbed. She was not herself at all. She was such a tearful, frightened little Lucy. She was not in the least like a Stoic.

'I am afraid not,' said Edgell. 'The Master has been failing for some time. The men all remarked that he would never read the Litany again in chapel.'

'You think he is so bad as that?' Lucy said tearfully.

'Yes, quite. Think of his age. His time must come some day, and he has lived longer than most men. You could not expect him, in any case, to live for many months longer.'

'No,' said Lucy sadly; and then he saw the tears dropping down her pale face. He could not believe she was weeping for that old, old man whose time had come, and who was a stranger to her till yesterday.

'What will you do when he is gone?' he asked abruptly.

'Do? I don't know—I have not thought. I shall stay at Newnham, I suppose, two years; I shall not be able to afford three; and then—and then I shall go out as a governess.'

'You shall never go out as a governess!' said Edgell with an oath.

Lucy looked at him, frightened and bewildered; she couldn't think what he meant, and then she broke down and began to cry.

'Dear Miss Rae—Lucy!' he said, and then he stopped and looked at the girl. He would have liked to take her in his arms, but there were several Newnham girls all hurrying down the road, and they looked at him, and they looked at Lucy. Some of them blushed, and some turned pale, and all were shocked. It was a dreadful precedent.

The atmosphere of Newnham revived Lucy, and she paused at the gate and looked up into his face with a little white smile.

'I am very stupid,' she said, 'but the Master frightened me so much, and I am not quite myself.'

He held her hand longer than he need have done, and he looked down into the small white face with a smile of ownership and protection that was quite new to Lucy. Nobody had ever looked in her eyes like that before, and, instead of drawing her hand away, Lucy hung her head and blushed like a poppy.

'Shall I bring you word how the Master is the first thing in the morning?' he said, still holding her hand; 'how early will you be out in the lane if I come?'

'Oh, as early as you like; seven o'clock!'

And so Lucy made her first appointment to meet Wyatt Edgell.

# CHAPTER XIII
# SLIPPING AWAY

When Lucy went out into the road outside the gates of the college, before seven o'clock the next morning, Wyatt Edgell was already there waiting for her. It is a short, narrow road, or lane, and it leads to nowhere, unless Selwyn College be considered anywhere. It has been the privilege of the students of Selwyn to use this road as a shortcut to their college, but it will not be their privilege much longer.

The road is now the private property of the authorities of Newnham, and a new wing connecting the old and the new halls will be built across the road, and the jealous walls that shut out the grounds from masculine eyes will be thrown down, and the old dusty lane will be covered with smooth, green turf, and it will be a thoroughfare no longer for the foot of man to pass over.

Perhaps they will restore again the old fortifications. There was a Roman camp here once, and a battle ditch running all the way to Grantchester. Every inch of ground here is classic, and strewn with remains of those old Romans who brought us all the gentler arts. Perhaps they brought the Muses with them and planted them at Newnham?

There was an old Roman dug up the other day, four feet beneath the surface, a noble skeleton, six feet six in length. The whole earth teems with ancient coins and pottery and Roman relics. They will have to build a museum in the new wing to preserve the 'finds' that are unearthed in digging its foundations.

Lucy was quite indifferent to the Romans. She would rather, if she had had the choice, have met one of their old ghosts in the lane than one of the Dons of Newnham taking her morning walk. She looked fearfully up and down the road when she got outside the gate, but there were only some Selwyn men going down to the bathing sheds; there was not a girl in sight.

Wyatt Edgell was walking up and down the path flicking at the sweetbriar hedge as he passed, and his eyes were looking down on the ground. He was so lost in thought that he did not see Lucy till he heard her little cry, and she ran to meet him.

'Oh!' she cried, a little pale and breathless, 'how is the Master? Is he worse this morning?'

She augured badly from Edgell's downcast look.

'Not worse,' he said; 'at least, I hope not worse, but I fear not better. When I inquired at the lodge when the gates were opened at six o'clock, they told me the Master had had a very disturbed night, that he had not slept at all, but that he did not appear to be in any pain. Your cousin has been up with him all night, and Mrs. Rae.'

'I was sure she would not leave him,' said the girl, the tears filling her eyes. She was thinking of the anguish in that kind old face when the Master slipped through her feeble arms. 'I think I ought to go over at once and relieve her; she must be worn out.'

Lucy didn't stay to think. She walked back to St. Benedict's with the undergraduate who had brought her the news; she didn't even stay to fetch her gloves. She walked down by his side in the morning sunshine, just as she had hurried out of her room, with a ridiculous little tennis-cap on her head and her ungloved hands. Two Newnham girls who were returning from an early—a very early—walk looked shocked, as well they might be, and some rude Selwyn men whistled as they passed. They were only jealous that she was not taking a morning walk with them.

Lucy found the watchers still up when they reached the lodge. Mrs. Rae would not be persuaded to lie down, and she was looking dreadfully tired and worn out. She looked ten years older, Lucy thought, this morning, and her poor face was as white as her hair. Mary looked pale, too. Perhaps it was the air of that close room that was still darkened; and there was a shade of anxiety under her eyes, but she would not own to being tired. She could stay up a week, if necessary.

The Master had fallen into a doze; but Lucy's light footstep or the whisper of their voices reached him, and he woke up when she came in. Lucy went over to him and laid her warm, moist hand on his, and the touch seemed to revive him.

'Is the milking over?' he asked, turning upon her his pale-blue eyes with that strange brightness in them that is peculiar to the very old. 'I have heard the cows lowing all night for the calves. You have taken the calves away?'

'It is Lucy, uncle,' she said, stroking his hand softly—'little Lucy, not Lucy's mother——' She was going to say 'grandmother,' but she thought 'mother' would humour his fancy best.

'Yes, yes: I know you, my dear. I have been watching for you all the night. You must not go away again for so long; they don't understand me here as you do. Where's Dick?'

'He is gone, uncle,' she said softly. She did not like to say that he was dead.

'Gone? Where is he gone? He was here just now. Is he in the field or in the barn? Send him to me when he comes in, my dear.'

Lucy turned away pale and trembling. She could not bear it; he did not recognise her in the least.

The Tutor came in while she was there, and went over to the bed; but the Master took him for Dick—the brother who had died fifty years ago.

His eyes lighted up when the Tutor came in, and with a strange, eager interest he asked him questions about the crops and the farm. All the later associations of his life had quite faded from his memory, and he had gone back to the scenes and faces of his youth.

The Tutor turned away from the bed with a sigh. He had waited for this half his life. He had looked forward so long as he could remember to being Master of St. Benedict's, and now, when it seemed within his grasp, he turned from it with a sigh. What was it, after all, this shadow he was grasping? Wealth, honour, position, it would all slip through his hands by-and-by, as it had slipped through the hands of the old scholar on the bed: all, everything, that had taken a lifetime—a long lifetime—to gain, would slip away, and there would be nothing left but old memories. Everything would fail; and he would go back to the old humble time, and the dear faces—if happily he had dear faces to go back to. There would be nothing left—nothing that he could carry away with him—but those old tender memories.

The Tutor turned away from the bed and went out of the room. On the landing outside he saw Lucy sitting in the window-seat weeping. The tears were in his own eyes, and he could not trust himself to speak. He went over, and took Lucy's hand, and drew her towards him.

'Oh,' she murmured through her tears, 'he does not know me the least bit. He thinks I am his brother Dick's wife.'

'And he takes me for Dick,' said the Tutor, with an involuntary smile, pressing the little warm hand he held. 'We shall all come to it, my dear, some day—to the vanishing-point, where everything slips away from us but the memories of our youth. Well for us at that time if we have nothing but innocent memories of kindly deeds and loving faces—if we have no regrets, no sorrow, no remorse! Perhaps it is the happiest lot to have the slate wiped clean of all the storms and passions of later years, and to go back at the last, and to take away with us only the memory of the old innocent early days.'

He was a good deal moved. He might have committed dreadful crimes since the days of his innocent youth, instead of being a grave, sober, reverend Tutor of a college.

'You don't think he will ever be better?' Lucy sobbed.

'I don't think, even if his life is prolonged, that his mind will ever be clear again. I fear it has gone, quite gone. Perhaps it is better so: he will pass away happier; he will have no regrets; he will leave nothing behind.'

Lucy sat sobbing in the window-seat. If she had been older she would not have wept so freely: the young have so many tears to spare.

'There is nothing to regret,' he said tenderly, bending over the hand he still held. 'The dear Master has lived his life—a good life, and, I think, a happy one—and he will exchange it for a better and a happier. We have only to concern ourselves about those who are left—Mrs. Rae and your cousin. They must stay with us, Lucy; they must make the lodge their home. You must let them understand, dear'—here the Senior Tutor really pressed Lucy's hand, that he had held all the time he had been talking to her, and she had never once thought of drawing it away: he would have taken her in his arms, but the servants were coming up and down stairs—'you must let them quite understand,' he went on, 'that their home is here with us. I am sure we shall do everything to make them happy.'

Lucy hadn't the least idea what he meant.

She would have stayed at the lodge and taken her share of the nursing night and day, but the Tutor would not hear of it.

'You have got your work to do, my dear,' he said. He called her 'my dear' now quite naturally. 'You have all your work cut out before you to be ready for the examinations in June. You can't afford to risk breaking down for the sake of doing work that any woman can do. A trained nurse from Addenbroke's will do all, and more than all, you three dear anxious women together.'

He sent in a nurse from Addenbroke's during the morning, and Cousin Mary and the Master's wife were turned out of the room. It was quite time the Master's wife was turned out of the room, or there would have been two to nurse instead of one.

The nurse who had been sent from Addenbroke's Hospital to nurse the Master was the little fluffy nurse that had been brought by her brother to Wyatt Edgell's rooms after that miserable folly, and had kept his secret.

If Lucy didn't like trusting a foolish young man she knew nothing about to this flighty nurse, she was much more unwilling to trust this valuable life in her hands. She watched with mistrust, and a certain dull glow of impatience, this little bit of a creature turn the Master's wife out of the room, and reverse everything that had been done under Cousin Mary's directions.

The nurse from Addenbroke's pulled up the blinds and threw open the windows, and let in the balmy air of the sweet May morning, that everybody had been so anxious to keep out; and she threw off the heavy quilts, and took away the pillows, and did everything according to the latest fashion in nursing. If people do not choose to get well when all this is done for them, it is their own fault, and not the fault of the system.

Before Lucy went back to Newnham she went into the little room—her own room till she had left it for Newnham—where the Master's wife had gone to lie down to rest. She had chosen this room because it was near the Master's, and she would be within call.

Lucy insisted on undressing her and putting her to bed, and perjuring herself with fibs of the deepest dye to set her mind at rest.

'I never thought he would go before me,' the dear old soul murmured, when Lucy was undressing her. 'I always thought I should go first; and it has been such a comfort to me to think that Mary could fill my place so well. And now to think that he should be called away first!'

'Who said he would go first?' Lucy said in her reassuring manner. 'He is not at all likely to go before you, you poor dear! If you had been yourself, he would not have fallen. You had no strength left, so he slipped through your poor arms. You hadn't the strength of a baby. Anyone can see how you have been failing lately, and you think it is the Master.'

'And you think it was my fault he fell—that the weakness was not in him?' the poor trembling old creature asked eagerly. She was so anxious to believe Lucy, and the faint colour flushed up under her white skin.

'Of course it was. The doctor will not tell you it was, because he doesn't want to frighten you. Anyone can see that you are much weaker than the Master.'

There really seemed some truth in what Lucy said. The Master's wife was trembling all over like a leaf—she couldn't have got into bed without Lucy's help; but she was trembling with joy.

'God bless you, my dear!' she said, when the girl went away. 'You have made me so happy!'

Lucy went back to Newnham with a heavy heart. It seemed as if everything were slipping away from her. It is so hard for the young to realize the great change. She felt dimly that it was not far off—that this was, indeed, the beginning of the end. Anyone could have seen that.

But it was not the personal sorrow of it that moved her; there was a deeper pathos than death in the fidelity of the dear woman who clung to the old Master with a love stronger than death itself. She could not but think of the look of relief on the old tired face as she walked back to Newnham.

The girls remarked that Lucy looked pale at Hall—that is, those who took any interest in her. Pamela Gwatkin never looked her way. She sat at the 'High,' among the Dons; she never condescended to look down the hall to the table where the freshers sat.

Capability Stubbs came into her room after Hall, as she sat trying to work, and brought her in a cup of tea. The tea was very grateful to Lucy's overwrought nerves: it was the only thing that was nice about Miss Stubbs. Pamela Gwatkin had given her a cup of tea once or twice, but it tasted of tooth-powder. She had packed the tea and the tooth-powder in a biscuit-tin when she came up, and the lid had got off the tooth-powder box, and it had got mixed up with the tea. It would not have been political economy to have thrown it away.

'Nice scandal you've been making in the college!' observed Miss Stubbs cheerfully, as she handed Lucy the teacup. She had only brought a teacup; she considered saucers superfluous, unless one happened to be a kitten.

'Scandal!' said Lucy, aghast. 'What scandal have I been making?'

'Oh! it was rumoured you had eloped with a Selwyn man. Somebody saw you going off.'

'With a Selwyn man!' said Lucy with fine scorn. 'As if I should elope with a Selwyn man! If it had been St. Benedict's it would have been different.'

'Or Hall?' suggested Miss Stubbs, who was rumoured to have a cousin at Trinity Hall, or to know a girl who had.

'Ye—es; even Hall would have been better. Who set the ball rolling—Newnham Assurance?'

Lucy was much too angry with Pamela to call her by her name.

'No, it wasn't Assurance. She took the other side. She said if you were going to run away with—with a man, you would have had the self-respect to stop and put your gloves on first.'

# CHAPTER XIV
# WYATT EDGELL

Late on the evening of the day when Lucy was supposed by the students of Newnham to have eloped, the man she was said to have eloped with sat working in his college-room.

It was not a Selwyn man. The crest on the pocket of the blazer he was wearing was the crest of St. Benedict's. It was nearly the eve of the Mathematical Tripos; there were only a few days more, and, having lost all the early part of the term, Wyatt Edgell was sitting down now at the last minute to recover by a tremendous effort the ground he had lost. He had always been sure of a first; he had never yet taken a second class in any examination at school or college, and his name had generally stood first in the lists. The authorities of St. Benedict's had predicted that it would stand first now in the coming Tripos.

There would have been no doubt about it but for that ugly 'accident'—he called it an 'accident'—in the beginning of the term. He had not been himself since he came up this May term. He had been moody and taciturn, and subject to fits of depression. He had given up his wine-parties, and his club suppers and breakfasts, and he had shut himself up in his rooms and sported his oak. Everybody, Tutors and all, said he was working hard, and they 'let him alone'; but his bed-maker knew better! Bed-makers know so much more about a man than anyone else.

She fetched Gwatkin to him one morning, when she had come in and found him lying on the floor in a fit of delirium tremens. They kept the matter quiet between them and put him to bed, and the bed-maker gave out to all the men on her staircase that 'he was a-readin' hisself to death.'

It was not a very bad attack—it was not the first, but Gwatkin didn't know that at the time—there were no violent ravings, only mutterings and depression—dreadful depression. Gwatkin and the bed-maker looked after him during the morning, and towards noon he fell into a deep sleep. It didn't seem at all likely that he would wake for hours. The bed-maker had had some experience of such cases, and she knew that the fever would take eight or ten hours' sleep to spend itself, and then he would awake with shaking hands and a splitting headache, and have a fine time of it for a week.

Leaving him as she thought sleeping soundly, she went about her work. She had to clear the tables of the other men on the staircase, but before she went she took the precaution to fasten his oak, and to take the key to Gwatkin's rooms.

Gwatkin ran over as fast as he could to Edgell's rooms. He had given such strict injunctions that he was not to be left alone on any pretence. Run as fast as he could, he was only just in time. Had he been a minute later he would have been too late. He took the razor from the poor fellow's hand, and he bound up the wound he had made with it as he best could without assistance. He had not the heart to call for help, to reveal his miserable secret to the whole college. He did for him as he would have wished others to have done for himself if he had been in his place. He kept his secret.

There was a man on his own staircase who had a sister a nurse at Addenbroke's, and when he had done all he could for Edgell, and fastened his arms down to the bed, Gwatkin ran across the court and brought Brannan over. He had to let him into the secret; there was no help for it. He saw exactly how matters stood. He was in his third year, and it was not the first time that he had helped to cover up an act of undergraduate folly. Brannan went away to fetch his sister. He could promise her silence. Phyllis Brannan was as true as steel; but in his haste and agitation he had left the outer oak open, and Lucy came in.

Wyatt Edgell's secret had been faithfully kept by these men and women. Only one of them had committed a breach of trust—Lucy had told Pamela. She couldn't help it, she explained, if she had had to die for it the next day; but Pamela had held her tongue. Not a soul in the college guessed his secret—his dreadful secret. Everybody looked up to him, and praised him, and expected great things of him—everybody but his bed-maker.

She knew something about that last orgie. She had helped to put him to bed, and she had cleared away the small sodas the next morning. She smiled when she saw him settling down to work on the evening of the day when he had brought Lucy to the lodge from Newnham. 'A lot of readin' 'e'll get through,' she said, shaking her head as she went down the stairs with her basket under her shawl. "'E'll be under the table, I reckon, when I come in in the mornin'.'

Eric Gwatkin was doubtful about him, too. He was more anxious about Edgell's Tripos than he was about his own Special. He couldn't rest before he went to bed without coming over and seeing if he was all right. He found his oak sported, and he had to knock a good many times before Edgell would let him in.

'Confound it — —' he began, and then he saw Eric and stopped. 'Oh, it's you, Wattles!'

He didn't say it very graciously, and Eric was sorry he had disturbed him. He really looked in working trim. He had thrown off his coat, and he was sitting in his shirt-sleeves. He wore a flannel shirt, and the collar was open and showed his white throat and chest, as it had showed it that day when Lucy leaned over the bed and put on the wet bandage. It showed, too, what it had not shown on that day, when a scarf was thrown over the throat—an ugly scar extending for some inches beneath the left ear. It was still purple and red and discoloured—a hideous livid mark on the beautiful white skin.

Eric shuddered when he saw it. The sight of it always made him shudder to think what a near thing it was—what *might* have been! He could not understand how Edgell could bear to see it in the glass, could bear to uncover it, that others coming in might see it.

'I am sorry to disturb you, old man,' he said, looking round at the work on the table, and the books lying open before Edgell. 'I only looked round to see—if—if you were all right.'

'To see if I had cut my throat again,' said Edgell calmly.

There was a shade of bitterness in his voice, and his lips curled slightly with amusement or scorn, or both. They were beautiful clear-cut lips, full and tender as a woman's, and they had a way of curving when he spoke. They never quivered, they curved; and his nostrils dilated. It was a strong face, with a massive square jaw, but it had these nervous tricks.

'Very kind of you, Wattles,' he went on with a laugh; 'but I'm not going to repeat that performance again—at least, not for the present. I'm going in for my Trip—and—and I'm going to marry Miss Lucy.'

Gwatkin's face fell.

'I don't think this is a time to talk of marrying,' he said, with a certain hesitation in his voice, and the cloud on his plain, homely face deepening. 'The poor old Master is dying.'

'So much the more reason to talk about it. Lucy will want a home. She won't be able to stay up at Newnham, she tells me; she will have no one but her cousin Mary when the Master is dead, and the old lady. I think I shall ask her to-morrow. I should like her to feel that she will not be left friendless when the end comes.'

'I should wait till after the exam., if I were you. I shouldn't let anything interfere with the exam. You will have all your life to marry in.'

Edgell lay back in his chair and laughed good-naturedly at his Mentor.

'Anyone would think, Wattles, that you wanted to marry her yourself.'

There was no occasion for that very common-place-looking young man to blush so dreadfully.

'I only meant to advise you for your good,' he said awkwardly, and then he went over to the door and said good-night; but when he reached the door, and he had the handle in his hand, he paused irresolutely, and looked across the room at the man with the scar in his throat leaning back in the chair. The scar was dreadfully visible in that light. It seemed to have a charm for Gwatkin. He couldn't keep his eyes off it.

'What's up?' said Edgell, seeing that he paused by the door.

Eric came back to the table where Edgell was seated, and laid his hand on his shoulder, a friendly, unmistakable grip.

'Dear old man,' he said in a broken voice, and the other could see that his foolish weak lips were quivering, 'you won't mind my speaking my mind to you; you will forgive what I say?'

'Fire away!' said Edgell; but he didn't look at Gwatkin, he looked at the opposite wall.

'Before you go any farther—before you ask Lucy Rae to marry you—pause and consider— —'

'I've already considered,' Edgell interrupted impatiently, and with his face still averted.

'You have not considered everything. You have thought only of yourself. You have not thought of her.'

'I have thought of her!'

'No, no; you have not thought of her in the way I mean. Bear with me, dear fellow. God knows I am saying this for your sake and hers. You have not thought of her as orphaned and friendless, having no one but you in the world, being bound up in you, having all her happiness dependent upon you. A little, tender, delicate creature, with no spirit of her own, who would suffer, and break her heart, and never complain— —'

'What would she have to complain of?' Edgell interrupted savagely.

'God only knows!'

'You—you think I shall go over the old thing again—that— —'

'Hush! For heaven's sake don't let us even suppose it! You haven't got to consider yourself in this matter, you have to consider her. Do you think it fair to ask her—to—to—forgive me, dear fellow—to ask her to risk it?'

Wyatt Edgell bowed his head.

'You have no faith in me,' he said moodily, with his head upon his breast and his brows knitted.

'I have every faith in you, dear fellow; but I want you to think of her. It is the chivalrous thing to do. Forgive me for saying it. Unless you felt that you could make her happier than any other man in the world—and—and ensure her happiness, you have no right to ask her to marry you!'

Eric Gwatkin was quite astonished at his own temerity—astonished and frightened. He was a weak, nervous, emotional fellow; he couldn't trust himself to say another word. His voice broke, and his eyes were clouded, and he was afraid he had said too much, and with a grip of Edgell's great muscular shoulder he went away and left him sitting in his chair, with his head on his breast, and that ugly scar gleaming like the dark blade of a knife across his white throat.